Praise for
Katya Balen

'A wonderful narrative voice'
Guardian

'If you have a middle-grader, or know one, or are
one … treat yourself'
Daniel Hahn, *Spectator*

'She's a force to be reckoned with'
Ross Montgomery

'I love Katya Balen's clear-eyed, poetic writing style.
She has a special ability to dig deep into the
emotional lives of the children she writes about; she
is always privy to their darkest thoughts, always on
their side'
Alex O'Connell, *The Times*

'[Writes] with the pen of a poet and the soul of
Mother Earth'
Liz Hyder

FOXLIGHT

Books by Katya Balen

The Space We're In
October, October
The Light in Everything
Foxlight

FOXLIGHT

KATYA BALEN

Illustrated by Barry Falls

BLOOMSBURY
CHILDREN'S BOOKS

LONDON OXFORD NEW YORK NEW DELHI SYDNEY

BLOOMSBURY CHILDREN'S BOOKS
Bloomsbury Publishing Plc
50 Bedford Square, London WC1B 3DP, UK
29 Earlsfort Terrace, Dublin 2, Ireland

BLOOMSBURY, BLOOMSBURY CHILDREN'S BOOKS and the Diana logo
are trademarks of Bloomsbury Publishing Plc

First published in Great Britain in 2023 by Bloomsbury Publishing Plc

A catalogue record for this book is available from the British Library

ISBN: HB: 978-1-5266-4044-4; TPB: 978-1-5266-4043-7;
eBook: 978-1-5266-4041-3; ePDF: 978-1-5266-4042-0

2   4   6   8   10   9   7   5   3   1

Typeset by RefineCatch Limited, Bungay, Suffolk

Printed and bound in Great Britain by CPI Group (UK) Ltd, Croydon CR0 4YY

To find out more about our authors and books visit www.bloomsbury.com
and sign up for our newsletters

To Miranda Prag, my wild almost-sister

Chapter 1

It is Sunday evening and Rey and I are hiding in the coat cupboard. It smells like feet and boot polish and coat wax and the weather.

I can hear Lissa calling and I sink back into the rails and let myself be swallowed by the scent of seasons. The wool scratches my skin like an army of tiny knitted ants but I don't wriggle away. I hold my finger up to my lips to make sure Rey keeps still but I don't need to worry because Rey hates Sundays just as much as I do.

Sunday evenings are bad for lots of reasons. One of them is that it's bath night, which takes about four years and the bathroom floor gets cleaner than most of us do.

Another reason Sunday is bad is that supper is leftovers night, which means cabbage and potatoes and something grey and gristly that might be mouse. We've never seen an actual mouse but Alice swears she got a tail in her bowl once. I always pick around the maybe-mouse with my spoon just in case and Lissa tuts because I'm wasting food. Rey always eats everything and says it's delicious.

Rey rolls in the pile of gloves and stares up at the dark ceiling. She's holding a book because Rey is always holding a book even when there's no light to see the pages. She holds them close to her chest like the words will seep into her bones. She knows a million things but she never really says them out loud because Rey doesn't like to talk that much. She can talk, even if sometimes Alex is mean and calls her a mute. She just doesn't feel the need very often and that's OK because I always know what she wants and needs and thinks anyway. Sometimes she'll burst open and she'll say something so brilliant and so true that it's like a firework or the sun appearing suddenly from the darkest sky. But that hardly ever happens. She's quiet and she's shy and funny and she's the best person in the whole world and even though I don't know many people I still know that's true.

I can hear the bath running and the mop squeaking outside. Or maybe it's Lissa catching mice for tea. Sunday sounds seep under the door and I try to pretend we're anywhere but a crumbling damp house filled with Found children and anywhere but on the edge of the misty wildlands and somewhere where we are wanted and somewhere where we belong. Rey turns the pages of her book.

I close my eyes tight and try to imagine. I dissolve my thoughts and I sink down and down into my mind and I am very nearly far away and somewhere else and somewhere better.

Imagine I whisper. *Imagine that we're on top of an icy cold mountain far away and it's just the two of us and* ...

But then the shadows shift and the light comes rushing in.

Chapter 2

I peer up as Lissa opens the coat cupboard door. The smell of the house streams in. Old cabbage and wet floors and too many children. She puts her hands on her hips like a cross mother in a storybook but she's not actually cross and she's not our mother and this isn't a story.

Up and out please, Rey. I can see you under those gloves, you know she says and I think maybe there's a little tickle of laughter in her voice but she's swallowing it down.

Rey sticks her head out of the pile and there are at least three gloves caught in her wild tangle of hair. She grins at Lissa and clambers out of the pile but I stay still as a statue.

Fen, you're not invisible Lissa says. *Out please or there'll be no tea left for you before the gannets have it all.*

Oh no not Sunday tea that would be awful I mutter but I pull myself out of the coats and Rey and I leave the lovely quiet dark of the coat cupboard and trudge down the corridor into the kitchen for mouse soup and letters.

That's the other terrible thing about Sundays.

We're meant to write to our mothers.

And Rey and I don't have one.

Chapter 3

Rey and I were found at foxlight. That's what Lissa tells us. Right at that very moment when quiet twilight met the dawn and the sun and the moon and the stars wove their light together and the orange streaks of foxes could be seen brushing against the awakening sky. We've never seen foxes but I somehow wake up every morning just when the day and night are shaking hands and I stare into the wildlands and as the light grows and spreads I feel like I belong.

It was deep dark winter and the marshes were frozen and glassy and showed the splintered sky. We were nestled in the dip of a valley right at the very edge of the wildlands. We were curled up small and quiet like question marks in a swirl of snow and orange fur and white teeth. Lissa nearly didn't see us because she wasn't looking for babies out there right at that wild untamed border. She nearly tramped right past but then she heard a mewl from a creature that almost definitely wasn't a fox. Lissa doesn't know which one of us it was and that makes me cross because things like that are important when your whole story is just a few seconds long.

Two tiny babies! One so cross and one so quiet. One with eyes like a summer sky and one with eyes as dark as boot polish but both with the most beautiful red curls. You! The last thing I expected to see, even when my job is collecting babies. But no one had called me to come and find you. It was luck, I suppose. Lucky for me, lucky for you.

You were curled up so tightly with those foxes. That's why you weren't turned to ice babies and frozen blue Lissa told us and I know she means that's why we weren't dead but she doesn't want to say it like that because she wants to be kind and she doesn't think Rey and I want the truth and she doesn't think we could cope because we're just children but Lissa doesn't understand a lot of things about growing up.

Lissa unwound us from the foxes' tails even though they snapped with those bright white teeth and they bit at her soft wrists and now whenever I glance at her skinny wrists I can see she has a luminous half-moon of pinpricks where their fangs found flesh. She bundled us into her coat and she stamped across the frozen marsh under a snow-filled sky and she took us back to the house and defrosted us by the fire and when we were pink and furious she knew we would be all right and we'd keep all of our toes.

Everyone here was left by a mother who was alone and in trouble and who couldn't look after them. The house is called the Light House because it's the only flickering glow in a wild and empty land and everyone knows how to find it. Its light guides the mothers towards it so they can leave their babies safely. But the difference is our mother didn't do that. She left us with the foxes.

Lissa gives all the children here names to try and make us all equal and all the same. But all the other children came with their names so they just get middle names. Lissa gave us first names too. She says they're fox names. Lissa says we all have names that link us to our beginning and our new life, to sew us all into the house and the folds of the family she makes and the family we had before. But everyone else got a name made in the mouths of their mother. Some of them were left actual treasures too. And every single one has a letter telling them their story printed in truth and words and ink.

Zaki's mother left him a locket filled with her face, and three pairs of handmade red socks. He won't let us read his letter. Zaki's middle name is Rain and the sky was pouring when he was left here.

Alex's mother carved his actual birthday on to a scrap of oak shaped like a heart. His letter is filled with how he came to be and how he came to be left and how his mother will come back for him when she can. Alex's middle name is February. The first yellow tips of daffodils were peering through the earth where he was found.

Jasmine's mother gave her a medal from a long-ago war and in her letter she told her all about her soldier father and his home far away across the blue-black seas. Jasmine's middle name is Winter. There was a frost when she was found.

Alice's mother gave her a silver necklace hung with a single silver leaf and a drawing of a family tree with branches spread like arms opening wide. Her middle name is Dandelion because there were spiky yellow suns dotted across the heathland as Lissa welcomed her home.

Robin's mother gave him his name sewn tight on to his blanket so it would never get lost. His letter tells him about the birds that sang when he was born and why she couldn't stay and listen to their song with him. Robin's middle name is Blue because the sky was blazing the day Marl scooped him up from the doorstep and carried him through our front door.

Everyone has their name and their letter and their mother's story about who they are and what they can be.

But when the foxes had slipped off towards the frosted horizon and Lissa unwrapped our thin grey blankets no story fell from its scratchy folds. She thought for a moment that it was there, because a torn scrap of paper fluttered to the ground like a feather. But when she picked it up she just saw a blur.

A charcoal swoop.

A black slink of a fox dusted across the page.

That's it.

Not a single word.

Just the scribbled shadow of a fox.

We don't have a mother. And we don't have a story.

Chapter 4

Some children at the Light House have found their mothers. They've sent letters full of bright words and they say things like *I can't believe we both like soup* and *I knew you'd find me one day*, and I want to shout that liking soup isn't special at all and why didn't *she* come back for *you*?

Rey likes the letters and she says things like *But wouldn't you want to know those things?* And I snort and say *No thank you*. Lissa puts the letters up on a board in the hall and I rage every time a new brass pin shines in the misty light curling through the windowpanes. Once I took the letters down and I wanted to burn them in the fire and watch the words glow bright and blackened until they curled into nothing but Rey grabbed my hand away and pinned them up again and they glowed pale against the wall and I hated them even more.

Whenever another baby is left on this ragged edge between the wild and the world everyone always wonders what their story will be and what they might have been left with and what they'll learn when they're big enough to know. It doesn't matter though. You're just as stuck here. It doesn't matter if someone has told you everything or nothing at all.

And I don't care that we don't have a mother. And I don't care that we don't know anything.

But Rey does.

Chapter 5

On Sundays Lissa tries to get us to write letters to our mothers. She doesn't post them or anything. She gets us to put them in special folders we decorated when we were small and stupid and didn't know any better. Rey's is beautiful, all swoops of colour and the careful edges of flowers and plants and animals she'd found in storybooks. Mine is mostly scribbles and spiky shapes that look like the fangs of some wild beast. But it doesn't matter. We haven't got anyone to write to so we don't bother. Rey sometimes tries to write a few lines but I laugh and I say I can tell her better stories and I try to grab the paper and she scrunches it up and I scrunch mine up and we have an indoor snowball fight instead.

Lissa is always trying to get us to write something and she says it's all about keeping connections and making your own story and today Robin says he's writing to his mother about how he's learned all the parts of a bird skeleton and he thinks that will make his mother proud because she loves birds and so does he. So I say to Lissa *Right well we were found wild with the foxes so shall I write and tell them I'm aiming to dig my own den and scavenge for food and run free across the marshes then shall I?* And she looked sad but I don't care. But the more I think about that letter the more I think that I would like to live its words and I imagine just me and Rey and the sky and the wild and it's perfect.

So while the others draw and write their stupid letters, Rey and I spin pencils on the table and she draws strange scribbly patterns in her special little blue notebook that Lissa gave her for all her words and drawings and it's much better than any stupid Life Book. We play tic-tac-toe and hangman until the night sky eats up the daylight and we can go. Lissa looks at our pencil games and rolls her eyes and says we should try to share our ideas just like everyone else. I draw a sketch of the house and Lissa smiles but then I sweep the lines of a dragon across the page and make it eat the roof and she rolls her eyes again. Robin finishes colouring in a starling and its feathers bristle and shine and it's ready to fly off the page and make its nest in the faraway trees.

As soon as we're allowed, Rey and I run upstairs to the girls' room as fast as we can without sliding back down the just-washed stairs. Lissa calls something after us but we don't turn round because if we do she'll make us clean the windows or read the little ones a bedtime story and both of these things are terrible.

The bedroom is in the tower, which sounds cool and actually is quite cool because we can see for miles and miles from our bright windows and the tower is how the house got its name. At its very top is a huge lamp that glows and spreads a soft still golden light out into the dark nights like a beam searching for ships and guiding them home and keeping them safe from the snarled teeth of jagged rocks.

Tonight the bedroom is cold but not cold enough to see my breath and there is no frost spangled on the windowpane so we'll be cosy in bed especially if we keep our socks on.

I sit on the lumpy mattress and look through the window glass to the wild world outside. I am always drawn to the wildlands. There is something in their foreverness and the way they stretch far away beyond where my eyes can find their end. I can see sweeps of trees and dark forests and I can see the sharp ridges of blue-skinned mountains and I can sometimes see the dirty brown of marshes that glimmer wetly in the gloom. Sometimes I think I see the snaking glitter of a river. The wildlands are everything. My favourite thing is to imagine what it would be like if Lissa had never found us and we hadn't frozen to death but instead we'd grown up wild and brilliant and alone. We would live the perfect story but it would be true and it would be ours. We'd live without bedtimes or letters or baths or mouse soup and we'd eat berries from a bush and sleep under the stars. We'd build campfires and nibble charred meat from bones and swim in the sparkling river and catch fish with our bare hands.

And so I tell Rey stories.

Chapter 6

Our light is the only light outside because we are too far away from anyone who would use one apart from Marl, and his cottage is tucked into a dip a mile away behind the house. There is endless blackness stretching and yawning as the night curls around the house. Even the stars are quiet tonight. For a moment I see through the dark into the world beyond and something flickers and flares. But when I blink it's gone and the night is swallowing the house whole.

OK says Rey and she's put her pyjamas on and I can see the moonbright strip of her ankles because they're too short now and Rey has always been smaller than me but maybe she's catching up. She is holding a book about stars and the night sky but she's marked her place and closed the cover so she's not going to read right away.

Let's play Imagine I say because she's waiting for me to say that. She nods and she starts to wind up our lantern. Will gave it to us when he left because he was sixteen and too old to be here any more. He said he'd buy us a better one with his wages as a mechanic, but he hasn't yet. This one is fine though and no one else has one so it's extra special. You have to turn a handle for ages and ages to get the bulb to flicker and breathe out a tiny glow but it's better than batteries because we'd never get Lissa to buy those for us. They're too expensive and there are never enough to go round.

Rey puts the lantern under the bed covers and I pull on my pyjamas so quickly that the waistband gives a little shudder and tears. I roll it over because I can get Lissa to sew it up for me tomorrow with a needle and tiny neat stitches that look like she was never there at all. I turn towards bed and the lit-up lump that is Rey and I see the moon suspended like a secret in the misty dark outside. The silver light gleams through to the roll of the hills and the dips and peaks of valleys and mountains that shift and change with the weather. This house is a lonely place sewn right on the edge of another lonely place. There is no one out there.

I scramble into bed. The sheets are slippery with cold but we make our own world under the covers and it's full of warmth and light and shadows.

Imagine whispers Rey and her face is a scrap of moonlight. She doesn't finish her sentence.

Imagine we were at the very top of a mountain in the heart of the wildlands I say but Rey shakes her head.

Imagine we were swimming in the river and the water was full of bright fish that moved around us like a swirling silver cloak I try but Rey shakes her head again. She doesn't want my wild stories. She wants our mother.

Imagine she was a gem collector I say and Rey nods so I carry on speaking in our warm world under the covers. I spin the story and I let it fill all the space between us and the darkening nooks and crannies as the lantern spits and sputters its dying light.

Imagine she was a gem collector and she was on a hunt for the famous Marsh Opal which could only be

20

found in the wet wildlands where the earth meets the sky. Everyone said it was a piece of the moon or maybe a fallen star and it was lost in the waters forever. It was worth more than any other gem in the whole world. It could cure the sick and turn stones into spills of rubies and diamonds. It was magic and it was real. But the marshes were dark and dangerous and they could suck you in and hold you tight. She was so brave and so daring.

I watch Rey as I tell her the story about our mother and how she found the Marsh Opal but other people wanted it so badly they'd do anything to get it. So she had to run and hide and she couldn't take us with her so she left us where she knew Lissa would find us. Rey glows as the words wrap around her.

Again she whispers and hugs her arms round her bony knees and leans into me. She's relaxed and wrapped in stories and lamplight. She loves to hear every scrap of story I can spin about our mother and she wants them all to be true even though they're all just magic and make believe. She never wants stories about our father and I don't have any to tell. Children here wonder and talk about their mothers, I suppose. They grew us. They grew us and gave birth to us and they knew us. Then they left us.

Give me an idea I say and Rey frowns and spins a cinnamon curl around her finger. I cut mine short with Lissa's kitchen scissors and she shrieked when she saw me but she said that was only because I'd done such a bad job and then she tidied it up around my ears for me.

Imagine she lived in the village and sold books? Rey says and the words rise at the end like smoke because she's not sure about this story and I shake my head. I don't like stories like that. I like to tell ones that are wild and weird and nothing like those boring letters everyone else has. Rey loves the stories no matter what. She lets herself believe every single word.

Imagine she was an explorer I say.

I've told this one so many times that its edges are soft and worn and the words have become old and crumpled in my mouth. I don't really want to tell it again. I just want to imagine us alone in the wildlands because whenever I tell those stories it feels like I am

22

whole. Just for a bit. But Rey doesn't like those stories as much.

Imagine she was an explorer I say again and Rey folds herself around me. This one is good enough. We build a mother from words and in the halflight of the world under our covers she takes shape and she might be real. Rey loves it when I make our mother come back for us. It's like I can carve a puzzle piece she's been missing all her life and for a few moments she's happy. So I mould our mother's shadow and compose her voice like music in the air as she says *My babies my babies*.

I keep telling the story of our mother until Rey's eyes close like petals in the moonlight and she slips into sleep. I turn off the lantern and we curl together like we always do and our breathing begins to match. I fall into the space between waking and dreaming and I imagine being tiny and just-born and the duvet above us is a snow-filled sky and that our beginning was different.

But it's just a dream and it's just words and it's just a story I tell to keep Rey bright and happy.

23

Chapter 7

I wake up in the empty foxlight just like I always do and I look out of the smeared glass pane by our bed. The sky is low and brushed with steel and the wildlands are hidden but I try to trace their familiar edges with my finger. I run the lines of the trees and the mountains and then I stop because there's something different. There is something moving. I am sure of it. A shape that moved and shifted away from my finger as I drew the tumble of grass that snakes into the beyond. A sloping twist of shadow. I grip the window sill and I press my nose flat against the burning cold of the glass but the mist rushes in and the light changes to morning and there is nothing there.

I roll over and I curl into Rey and I try to go back to sleep but the shape moves darkly behind my eyelids.

Chapter 8

In the wild light of morning Rey is outside feeding bones to her garden. I am outside watching even though it's freezing cold and the mists are grey and low and starting to whisper inside my skin. There's nothing else to do today unless you count playing cars with Zaki or playing cards with Alice or listening to Robin plink through a song on the piano or stomping up and down the endless corridors to try and keep warm because there's not quite enough wood to light the fires all day long and Lissa only puts the big metal radiators on when it's a special occasion. I am going to be cold inside or outside so I might as well keep Rey company. It's always better to be near Rey, and it's always better not to be playing cars with Zaki.

Rey throws handfuls of ground bone powder on to the wet soil and it glows like stars in a blue-black sky.

The air is damp and heavy and Rey's clothes are sticking to her skinny body. I can see the thread of her spine like a row of cotton reels and the bones of her wrists as she scoops more bone meal from her bucket. She kneels down right in the mud and sprinkles carefully. Her fingers are glowing white and blue. Rey will never put on gardening gloves and she says she needs to feel the earth with her fingertips and that the cold doesn't bother her one bit. She always wears her favourite yellow hat but that's because Lissa knitted it and she loves it and not because it keeps her toasty warm. I wonder if not feeling the cold is something to do with being found iceblasted and snowsoaked but I can't stand the cold so it can't really be that. I sometimes think the ice never melted from my bones and all the sharp shards are still trapped inside me.

Rey pokes at the dark earth with a purpling finger. Nothing ever grows in this soil. It swallows everything Rey puts in and spits out nothing in return. She writes down the seeds she's planted and the weather that day and some other little things in her blue book as if that will make a difference and somehow the flowers will bloom because of her diligent notetaking. But she really doesn't seem to mind either way. She's not bothered when things aren't perfect. If we lived in the wildlands I'm sure her flowers would grow. I would tangle them through our hair and wear them like crowns and we'd be queens of all the wild.

I wander through the icy garden. The rabbits shift and hop in their hutches and a few sit in the wire run and sniff the air. It's probably too cold for them to be outside now and so soon Lissa will make us carry their heavy wooden homes into the boot room. Robin loves the rabbits. They were his idea and he begged and begged until one day Marl turned up with a cage slung in the back of his truck and six pairs of bright eyes glowing in the morning sun. He wouldn't tell us where he'd got them from but I don't think it was easy. Quite soon after we had a lot more than six pairs of eyes and so Marl built another rabbit run. One for boys and one for girls. Just like in the house.

Rabbits in the wildlands would run free.

The Light House is built on the very edge of the wildlands and the world. No one lives out beyond us.

They are snug and safe in the tiny town and scattered in the villages that are dipped in valleys below and we can never see their lights or their people. Marl is the closest person to us and we hardly ever see him unless Lissa needs something fixing and she can't do it herself. This house is a full stop and nothing comes after. Except it has to. It's where we were found and so there must have been someone there. There must have been something. I spend a lot of time looking out to the flat horizon and a lot of time seeing nothing.

But something catches the corner of my eye. Over by the wire and wood of the rabbit hutches. A burst of orange flame. A flicker. A tiny moment of colour and movement. I see its shadow rise and fall and a paintbrush streak of colour spread itself through the grey. The same sloping movement I saw early this morning, I'm sure of it. I whirl round and try to follow but there's nothing anywhere except endless sky reflected in the wildland waters.

Same as always.

Chapter 9

Rey is taking forever with her digging and her scraping and her gentle mutterings to soil that never listens. Rey is full of light when she gardens and she glows when we play Imagine and especially when we imagine our mother. She doesn't want to leave the Light House and see what's beyond the snaking wire fence and out towards the wide wild world that stretches on and on towards the painted horizon. The wildlands would take care of us just like they did when we were babies. They are better than mothers and letters and all the things the others have that we don't. It feels like they belong to us. But Rey is waiting for our mother to come here and find us. She won't leave with me and follow the goldengrass paths into the heart of the wild because then our mother won't know where we are. She doesn't know where we are anyway but Rey always says she would work it out. But she's not coming back. It's just a story Rey likes to hear me spin.

Thinking about the wildlands makes me feel like I'm alive more than any Imagine game ever could.

They call to me. They feel real and true. They're where I belong. That's where our story started, out there in the frost-dipped grass with the foxes curled around our tiny kicking legs. We are a part of them and I want to explore their dips and peaks and touch the sky at the very top of a mountain. It's where we started and they're our beginning but they're more than that to me. They feel like they're an extension of me, like my blood runs through the river and my bones have been built into trees and hilltops. It's hard to explain. Even Rey doesn't understand, and we share everything. Except this.

I huff out a plume of airsmoke that disappears into the mist before I can even watch it twist into a new shape. I try again but the mist grabs hold of my breath and I give up trying to make my air dance in the sky. I watch as it blows across the land, a tiny part of me mingling with the wild. I can feel my eyes starting to tingle and burn and I blink and blink and blink before tears can escape because I won't let that happen. The landscape blurs into a streaked painting. I curl my fists. I push down the longing. I take deep breaths. And when my eyes clear I am sure I see Rey staring at me but in an instant she is back to raking furrows in her soil.

I crouch in the soil next to Rey but I don't sit because it'll make my trousers damp and also Rey will tell me off for squashing her seeds. I thumb the soil and keep my face turned away from her.

I'm about to coax her back into the smokywarm of the house when the air explodes with a sound that cuts right through me.

A scream.

It isn't coming from Rey and it isn't coming from anyone in the Light House because it's outside here with us and it is jagged and it shatters the sounds around us until there's nothing but the sound and it pierces me and it's inside me and I am nothing but the endless endless scream. I've never heard anything like it and it makes me want to curl up and cover my ears and never hear another sound ever again. It fills every inch of the misty air and it is bigger than the sky and it pushes up against the clouds and gets louder and louder.

Then the door of the house bursts open and all the others fly out into the soft morning mist and I unfreeze.

And I see the blood.

Red and rich and soaking through the hungry earth.

Chapter 10

The rabbit is dead. Its eyes are pooled with a sky it can't see. Jasmine spots the dark red spill of blood at its neck and starts to cry. The baby wails and both of their sounds are so different to the scream that split the air.

Who screamed? asks Alice and she looks around and I know she's counting all of us just in case. Rey steps a little closer to me and I find her hand and hold it tight.

The rabbit says Robin because he doesn't just know about birds. He picks it up and we all screech and step back but Robin pours the tiny body through his hands like water. He runs his fingers along its fluid fur and he finds the bloody space where the teeth went in.

Something tried to kill it to eat it he says and he

33

strokes the rabbit's burned brown brow as if it needs to be soothed into sleep. *Snapped its neck and bit its throat. I wish I'd seen.* He keeps holding the tiny body and he's taking in every detail of its spiked fur and its velvet ears. The other rabbits look on and they're frozen with the horror of it all.

Alice shudders.

We interrupted whatever wanted it says Robin and he lays the rabbit gently on the ground but away from the pen. *I'm going to leave it here. Waste not want not.*

Jasmine looks a bit like she might be sick.

Rey is staring at Robin and I can see the sky in her eyes too.

A *fox did this* she whispers to me and the shocks and the shouting are forgotten because this is so much bigger. Her words slide out slowly and they are so quiet that no one else can hear them. It's not a question really but I know she wants me to ask it out loud so I do.

Could be says Robin. *Foxes will eat anything they can. Never seen one here though* he says and he closes the rabbit's terrified eyes with his thumb. *Poor Bertie.*

I sniff the air and something musky and sour and deep floods my nostrils. It is horrible and it is comforting and it's a memory that shifts and swirls like mist and I can't grab hold of it.

Then Lissa comes out in a rush of worry and crossness and she sees the blood and our pale faces and she panics before she even sees the rabbit and then she holds her hand up to her mouth and closes her eyes.

Are you all all right? Is everyone OK? she says and the notes of her voice are high and they are carried away into the wind. She looks down at the rabbit and she sees the broken neck and the tunnels where the teeth found bone and blood and gristle and she shakes her head. I roll my eyes and mutter that it's just a dead thing and everything ends up dead eventually but Lissa is too busy checking everyone has all their fingers and toes.

Inside, everyone she says. *Inside and away from this now*. She takes the baby out of Alice's arms and she walks back towards the Light House and we follow like ducklings and leave the death behind.

35

Lissa wraps the rabbit pen in wonky layers of chicken wire that bites her fingers and then she comes inside and makes hot sweet tea for the shock of the blood and the body and she kisses the tops of all our heads and tickles the baby under his arms until he shrieks. Jasmine and Alice cry a bit about the dead rabbit even though they never really pay the rabbits much attention. But everyone else is excited and they tell the story over and over until it turns into Robin tackling a wolf with his bare hands and saving all our lives. Robin doesn't correct this version and he looks up wolves in one of his books and reads out facts about them to anyone who will listen. Alice says she'll never go outside again and Robin says she never goes outside anyway and Alice says there's nothing to do outside so why would she go outside and the whole conversation loops round and round in a circle until I want to scream like the rabbit. I keep thinking about charcoal drawings and red blood and the fox and the wildlands where it came from.

Lissa tells Robin not to pick up dead things again *please* but he just shrugs and says next time he might keep it so he can study its bones and its brain and that if you take out an animal's lungs you can breathe into them with a straw and watch them inflate like balloons even though their air can go nowhere at all any more. Jasmine shrieks and I press my face into the kitchen table and the world goes dark but it doesn't go quiet. I feel a weight on my shoulders and I think it's Rey burrowing into me but it's Lissa's soft arms around me and she kisses the top of my head and she tells me *It's all OK now, it's all OK*. But I wriggle away because I don't need someone to tell me that.

Lissa goes off to help Zaki set up a den in the living room and make sure Jasmine does the sweeping and Alex does the mopping and to make sure the baby has some rusks and then a million other busy things that Lissa always has to do and I should help with.

Shall we make breakfast? I say because suddenly I'm starving and my tummy growls and stretches and I think of the fox again. Rey nods and so I light the big stove, even though Lissa doesn't allow us to use fire when she's not around. It only takes me five tries and eight matches, which is better than last time and I've still got all my eyebrows. My hands were trembling because the snapjaw of fox on rabbit is the very wildest thing I've ever known, the death and the blood were an icewhite shock and I can still feel it pulsing through me. I heat up porridge over the blue iceberg flame and Rey drops raisins into the pan. At the very last second I stir in fat lumps of brown sugar. This is exactly how we make the perfect porridge and it's our secret recipe although sugar and raisins aren't exactly secrets. We're not supposed to use them but I can climb up to the highest shelf now and Lissa doesn't know.

My hands start to steady and the blush of blue is slowly fading from Rey's skin. There is earth in the seams of her fingers and a single leaf in the curl of her hair. She rubs her hands together and stares out of the kitchen window at her dark garden as if suddenly green shoots will start to jump out of the soil and surprise her. I look outside too but I'm not watching for the sprouting of seedlings.

The sugar melts and smells delicious and before

long some of the others are wandering back into the kitchen. Nothing is ever really your own in the Light House. Everything is shared and it never feels like something truly belongs to you. That's why I keep my drawing pencils under my pillow and my lantern next to my sleeping head and it's why Rey's pockets are always stuffed with seeds and notebooks.

I serve everyone a hot steaming bowl of sugary porridge and they sit round the table and squabble and make a racket. But I am curled up on the huge sill staring out of the window and so is Rey and so is Robin. We watch and wait and my blood starts to poke and sting and needle my skin because I've been sitting still for so long. The leftover porridge cools and concretes my bowl and Lissa will be cross.

Seconds slide into minutes and hours but we don't move a muscle. The mist is thickening and growing darker and soon we're missing a Snakes and Ladders tournament and hot buttered toast and Lissa's stories by the fireside but we don't move.

This feels too important.

Then we see it.

A shadow falling. A movement like water.

A fox slides through the mist.

It pounces on the dead rabbit's dulling fur and Robin and Rey gasp together in one breath but I am too busy staring to breathe and even my heart might have stopped beating because this is too astonishing and incredible and brilliant. A fox.

We have never seen a fox before.

It lifts its sharp face up and sniffs the air. Then it dips its beautiful head and pads back into the wildlands with the limp rabbit pressed between its jaws.

It pauses just before the blurred edge between us and the land that stretches far away into a whole new world and then it turns back and it looks right at me with those eyes that are full of wild and otherness.

I feel like I'm looking at something I have known forever and something I don't know at all. It's like a golden thread of light is spinning out from my chest and right into the eyes of this wild and beautiful creature and we are joined and connected by something fragile and strong and strange and familiar.

40

The fox is freedom.

I squeeze Rey's hand and she turns to me and she is full of wonder and her eyes are burning bright with something I have never ever seen there before.

Chapter 11

I know Rey is turning what's happened over and over and inside out and upside down.

A fox has come to the Light House.

What does it mean? asks Rey and that look is still sketched on her face. I think it means something very different for Rey than it means for me.

I want to tell her that it doesn't mean anything and what could she possibly think it means anyway, but I can't. Because once I say it she'll let the words sink down deep inside her and she'll lose the spark that's now lit in her belly. She's so full of light and brightness. I've never seen her like this before and her light bounces into me too.

She's borrowed one of Robin's books and she's searching the pages and she's frantic to find the right words. Every so often she'll read out a phrase and the words flow from her like a river. Her excitement is electric. The sun has slid across the whole sky and the moon is peering from the clouds but she's still looking.

It doesn't make sense she says, and it might be the millionth time and I love Rey and I love it when she speaks and how seeing the fox has made all her thoughts come loose and spill into the space between us but right now I want to chuck her out of the window so I can get some sleep. *Have you seen this bit, Fen? You should read this bit, you'd love it. Why wouldn't the foxes have eaten us? Why has this one come back now? What does it mean?*

I don't know I say for the millionth time but there's no point because she's not listening.

It definitely means something she says and she turns another page. *It's a clue.*

What do you mean, a clue? I say and I think about how detective stories are about magnifying glasses and stolen jewels and not foxes and mothers.

Because they didn't eat us she says. *They kept us warm they kept us safe and and and* and her face is

43

faraway and dreamy and she doesn't finish her sentence because her mind is rushing too quickly. This is how she looks when I tell her stories about our mother.

I should tell her that I sort of understand, even if it's for different reasons. I should tell her that I don't want to chase off into the wild in search of something that might not be there but because of something that definitely is. No more mouse soup and letter-writing Sundays and screams at bath time and mopping the floors. Bright wide skies and a canopy of stars and air that tastes like earth and flowers and life. I should tell her I want to understand more and I should tell her about that sudden golden moment I saw the fox slinking towards us on soot-dipped paws. That the fox is everything I want and need. Running free, looked after by nobody, no questions, no answers. Wild.

But I can't find the words either.

That night we get ready for bed in the chilled bedroom but instead of diving under the covers straightaway and making a warm cosy nest with Rey curled around me, I look out of the window and I look into the night. I don't see the slink of a fox but for a moment I think I see a tiny light pressed tight against the horizon. But as I turn to tell Rey, it disappears and it must have been a star behind the shifting mists.

And so I get into bed and I whisper *Imagine*.

Imagine we followed the fox.

Imagine.

Chapter 12

The next day Lissa calls Marl to come and make the garden and the hutches safe because she wants to make sure we don't lose any more pet rabbits and also she heard a story about foxes coming into a house and baring their sharp white teeth and she's worried. There are already fences around the Light House and I'm never sure whether they're to keep us in or keep something out and they're very old and they shiver in the wind.

I try to ask Lissa about foxes but she isn't in a listening mood because Zaki has a pea in his nose and Marl is about to arrive and no one has had any breakfast. I stomp off without helping and my feet make the wooden floorboards shake and the baby cries until Rey picks him up and spins a toy in the air until he laughs so much his chubby cheeks tremble.

Marl appears through the mists in his bright red truck that is always full of things we're not allowed to touch or he shouts. I can see the sharp teeth of saws and twists of wire and dull metal boxes that I want to open but Marl scares me just a bit too much to be sneaky. He swings open the truck's door and it claps shut with a bang that scatters the crows from the trees.

Marl starts unwinding rolls of chicken wire and unpacking his rusty toolbox. He lays out everything he'll need in perfect order. Marl doesn't like it if you swap his tools round when he's working. Jasmine found that out last time and now she's hiding upstairs in case he sees her.

Marl is patching holes in the fence that wraps us up and keeps us away from the wilds. Lissa said she had chickens once but they were eaten in the night and all she found in the morning were empty feathers shuddering in the morning air.

I'm angry because Marl is trying to keep away my one connection to the wild. I would give anything to see the fox again. Rey is worried because she thinks Marl will damage her bare garden and she tugs on my

47

sleeve because she wants me to tell him to be careful, but she heard him shout at Jasmine and Rey doesn't even like talking to friendly people. I think it's basically bonkers to care about empty soil but Rey is jittering on her toes and twisting her fingers so I say *OK OK* and we go out through the back door.

Marl is kneeling in the soil and hammering posts into the soft ground. He doesn't look up and see me standing in the halfshadow of the porch because he's concentrating on fences and wires. His tongue is poking between his teeth and every time he brings his mallet down I worry that he'll bite through it and feed the earth with his blood. Lissa is standing nearby holding the baby and jiggling him so he doesn't cry in the cold air.

There are just so many things to worry about, and I'm sure it would be fine without all this but you just don't know, do you Lissa is saying as she puts a finger on the baby's fat red cheek and strokes warmth into him. He babbles at the sky and she smiles at his sounds.

There are too many of the blinking things if you ask me says Marl and his voice is muffled and gruff and low.

48

Or there was when that barefoot wilder lot was up in those blinking wildlands anyway, camping and getting themselves involved where they weren't wanted. Then we end up with these blinking things, snapping and stealing and getting into everything. I said those animals would come down to the houses if they didn't stop and I was blinking right wasn't I. That blinking woman used to feed them, the wild one, no shoes, wandered the wildlands with the rest of those nutters. Raw chicken and eggshells all over the place. Then they came looking for it. Came into our places, didn't stay outside where they belong. You can't tame a blinking animal. Makes them useless and soft.

I'm not sure we can blame that lot says Lissa and she jiggles the baby and the way she says *that lot* is a lot softer than the way Marl said it. *This is the first fox I've seen in a very long time. Not since before the wilders left. I don't think they were trying to tame things anyway, were they? They were trying to make it all wild again. Bring it back to life.*

Marl grunts and hammers another post and spits in the soil and straightens up and my heart is an animal roaring in my ribs.

49

Chapter 13

A woman.

Wild one.

No shoes.

Feeding the foxes.

I turn to Rey and her eyes are bright and dancing.

Our mother she whispers and her words are carried
away into the mist.

Chapter 14

Rey is bouncing and bold and she is the most alive I have ever seen her and all her edges are sharp against the mist. I can see her standing next to the house and for the first time I can see her pulling away from it. Pulling towards something else. I am trying to calm her down but my own thoughts are wild and so is my heart. I can feel the newness and the shock and the excitement crackle through me like electricity. This is our chance.

Rey is tugging at my sleeve again and at this rate I am going to have one jumper arm longer than the other and this is the only jumper I own.

We step out of the shadows of the doorway and walk over the soft damp earth. Lissa has walked off with the baby and she's showing him the way the mist sparkles if you look at it just right. *Look at the lights, baby, look at the pretty lights* she sings and the baby claps his fat hands.

Marl shifts some of Rey's precious soil and she squeaks but she doesn't say anything because she can't. Marl doesn't hear because his ears don't work like they should any more. He doesn't notice us until our shadows throw themselves across his hammer.

What? he says and he makes a short word sound even shorter.

I take a deep breath because this is the moment we'll know. I didn't think it would be like this. I didn't think it would be in Rey's bone-scattered garden and I didn't think it would be Marl who would twist open the lock and let our story burst free and I didn't think I would be so very scared to know. I didn't think I cared about anything except the wildlands and Rey. But this is for Rey, I think. This is what she wants.

The woman who fed the foxes I say and my words are tiny.

What? says Marl again and the air ripples with his annoyance.

The woman who fed the foxes I say again and I make it sound bigger.

Yeah he says and hammers in a post. The sound echoes off the sky. A faraway unseen crow calls an alarm and I want to run and tell Robin and not have to stand here in front of Marl with my boots sinking into the soil.

Talking to Marl is like slowly unwrapping a present, except the wrapping paper is a grumpy man holding a hammer. I squeeze Rey's hand.

Who is she? I say and then *Who was she where is she where can we find her can you tell us about her?* and it's all flooding out of me in a tumble and I'm surprised how easily I find the questions that I've never wanted to ask. Rey is holding her breath and I can hear the creak of her lungs as she keeps them steady and still.

Her? I don't blinking know, do I. Disappeared. Went off into the wilds again. Or went home to her mammy. None of my business.

Which one? I say because those two things are very, very different.

53

What? he says again and I squeeze Rey's hand so hard that she breathes out in a huge rush of air that turns the space around us smoky.

Which one did she do? I say. *Did she go home or did she go into the wilds?*

I don't know, girl. Maybe it was neither. Maybe it was both. Maybe she went off to join those blinking dreamers in the marshes planting all that nonsense and encouraging all those blinking animals. Maybe she went and got herself a nice job in a library. Funnily enough, she didn't think to tell me and I didn't ask.

I open my mouth to ask another question but Marl brings down his hammer with a crack and turns away.

Please says Rey and Marl jumps because her voice slices through the damp air like a diamond cutting glass. *Please tell us more. Please.*

I look at Rey's hopeful, desperate face and my heart cracks.

Marl rubs a knotted hand over his crumpled face.

I don't know he says and he is more gentle now but there is still a sharpness to his edges. *I really don't. There was a group of them once, load of blinking* barefooters. Wilders, they called themselves. Living out there, doing God knows what. Thought they could bring it all back to life. Those lands been dead longer than I've been alive. Foolishness to try and bring 'em back. Probably why them lot aren't there any more from what I hear. No one comes back from the wildlands. They swallow you whole. But that's the only thing I heard, and who knows what's true and what's not. All I know is that she brought those blinking foxes right to my door and I lost sixteen chickens. Good riddance to her. Now leave me alone.

And we do.

Chapter 15

She disappeared into the wildlands says Rey and her eyes are full of a whole new world and her words slip out smoothly because she's not really here right now. She's drifted off into the wildlands and into the story of our mother. *She lived out there. She planted things. Just like me. She was a wilder. Just like you want to be.*

And I can almost see our mother printed on her face and the roots of our story starting to creep and grow and bloom.

A wilder. I turn the word upside down and inside out and try to understand the shape of it. A wilder. Trying to bring the land back to life. Trying to make it grow. Trying to make it wild again. I feel a sudden rush of love for the word and everything it means. But I try to squash the feeling because I know there's no point in getting giddy with it and have everything fall to pieces.

We don't know that she's our mother I say but I watch the cracks start to spread on Rey's face as my words pull her away from the story and away from what she wants to believe. I can't do that to her. So just for a moment I let myself be part of the story too and I think about the moment I saw that fox dip its cinnamon head and look back at me and slip into the mists like a ghost. Rey is right. The fox is a message. It's just saying different things to each of us.

We have to find her says Rey. *We have to go.* And her words come out in jerks and scattered sounds. I feel a ripple of something that might be fear and might be joy and it bursts under my skin like sparks. Rey is never like this. She is quiet and she is part of the background and she is never the one asking for anything. Rey looks to me for the answers instead of being the one to ask questions and she looks to me to say all the words that get tangled inside her. We've swapped round and I don't feel like myself. I'm the one who has always wanted to step into the strangeness of the wildlands and never come back. Rey has always wanted to stay the same and stay safe.

We can't I whisper. *We don't know how* and I can't believe I'm suddenly nervous and pulling away from everything I've ever wanted. The chance to leave and to start again. To go back to our beginning. To stop telling stories that can never be true and to start our own story somewhere we belong. Somewhere that fits and where we can be wild and ourselves and not have anyone looking after us and telling us what to do.

She sent that fox to find us says Rey and her words are careful and clear.

Rey is bright and determined and alive and the story of our mother is filling her with a light I have never seen glow inside her before. I can feel its warmth shine on me and I want to keep her bright and I squash down the wriggling niggles that slither in my mind like snakes.

So we start to plan.

Chapter 16

I don't believe the fox was sent for us by our mother. Of course I don't. We're just playing Imagine. It's something I would tell Rey to make her glow and curl into me and ask for more stories that can't be true but make us feel like we're part of something big and exciting, but that afternoon when she asks for the story it starts to fit in my mouth and it flows from me and I find the right words and they colour the air around us until I've painted the fox from my mind and we can see its brightbrush tail sweeping through the night. The story starts to feel like I can touch it. I can see scratchy berry bushes full of fat fruit. I can imagine biting into their soft flesh and letting them burst in my mouth but I can't find the flavour. I can feel my fingertips brush up against the shadow of our mother and she's solid for the first time ever and my heart trembles but as soon as I think it she is swallowed into mist and dust and I shake my head because it's not true. It's not true and there's no point thinking it is.

I just have to pretend for Rey, just for a bit. Just until we're out there.

We wait until the strange yellow daylight is fading into the clouds and the moon is struggling to glow in the mist. Lissa has bathed the little ones and read them stories and the house is quiet and gentle. We wait until she's gone into her office and then we tiptoe downstairs and creep around in the dark like spies or ghosts. We have to pack so we're ready and we're waiting and we can go as soon as we see the fox. I want to go immediately but Rey says we have to wait and we have to follow.

We won't know which way to go she says and I say *I will*. I might never have put a toe into the wildlands but when we get there I will know them. I will know what to do and where to go and they will be as familiar to me as the lines on my palms and the curve of Rey's face.

60

We sneak through to the kitchen and I take food that I hope will last. Heavy bread and yellow cheese wrapped in an oily cloth and big slices of salty cured meat and a bag of oats and raisins and sugar lumps. I steal two metal mugs meant for little clumsy hands and a tiny saucepan and I hope we can find a way to have our tea and porridge in the wild. I feel a bubble of guilt burst inside me because everything we take is something the others can't eat, and Zaki loves cheese and Alice eats dried meat like a tiger.

I take a big metal bottle and fill it with water. I wrap everything up tight in a tablecloth so nothing will clank and clang when I put it in a backpack, but the weight surprises me. I empty the bottle. We'll find water on the way. But Rey shakes her head and she fills the bottle again and shows me how she'll tie it round her waist with twine. Sometimes I forget how nimble her thin fingers can be and how clever she is. She remembers to take matches and more twine and a small knife with a handle that shines like a pearl.

We go upstairs with the backpacks Lissa wears when she goes to collect a Found baby. Rey folds clothes into the bags like she's feeding a hungry animal. I pack Will's lantern so we'll have light in the dark. We lay out our warmest, heaviest clothes, ready to pull them on as soon as we know we have to go. My winter jumper feels scratchy and itchy like it always does because the person who made it wanted to do enough so they didn't feel guilty when they thought of us but not so much that they had to think of us much at all. It is lumpy and the arms are unravelling. I make sure we have thick socks and some pants but not loads because I don't think changing pants will be that important in the wildlands. I add lots of vests because being warm is the most important thing. I find Rey's yellow hat under the bed and I know Lissa knitted me a red one but I don't know where it is and I hate it because I look like a tomato in it but it would be quite useful in the wildlands. I do find two scarves though and I am ready to wrap myself up like a parcel. Rey adds her notebook and my drawing pencils and her ancient book about gardening to the bag and I almost say something but I stop myself. She folds our little charcoal fox drawing into the pages of her notebook and packs it too and it feels right.

When we have packed we sit and we wait. Rey presses her nose against the windowpane and leaves ghostly smears of her face on the glass but the night is still and silent. We sit up together and we curl together and we wait and we wait and we wait but when the sun rises pinkly through the fog and disappears behind a ceiling of clouds we are both asleep and dreaming and in my dreams I believe and the dream makes me whole.

Chapter 17

The next morning when I wake from my dreams in the empty foxlight Rey is curled in a tight ball beside me. We get up and we don't need to get dressed because we slept in our outside clothes and I don't bother washing my face or brushing my tangled hair and Lissa says I look wild and I want to bite back with sharp teeth and words. Rey and I are tired and cross and the rucksacks under our bed smell like sweating cheese.

We bicker and fight and we play cards and I win and Rey throws hers on the floor and I shout and she shouts back and then the whole day is misery. The sadness smooths our sharpness and we stop throwing words and toys and fury and we sink into the soft feeling of hopelessness.

We are flat for the whole day. Flat as the pancakes Lissa makes because it's the baby's first Found Day and so he gets a special supper. We should stop calling him the baby and start calling him Inigo because that's his name even if it is a bit weird. The baby is too big to be a baby any more and he can nearly walk although he never has to because someone always wants to carry him and show him the world. He is the littlest and the sweetest but only for now because there will always be another.

Inigo eats two pancakes and bangs his spoon for more and after he eats his third he's sick down his front and then he cries and then he laughs when he's given a bath in the sink so it's all a very normal supper. But Rey and I aren't really there. We are just outlines and we fade and blur in the chaos and the noise.

We sit and we say thank you for the pancakes and we all clap and we tickle Inigo under his wet chin and Lissa kisses the top of his soft head and the warm fire makes the room glow. I have a tiny feeling for a tiny second that's so small and fast that it blows away like the dust bunnies that nestle in corners of the pantry. But when Lissa tries to kiss my head too I duck away and she's left with nothing but air.

We give Inigo a present of a drawing I did a few weeks ago before foxes and wilders and packed bags. I've drawn a bird in flight and it's supposed to be a lark but I don't know what a lark looks like and Robin was being huffy because he's the ornithologist and wouldn't share his books, so I just guessed and it's a swooping purple bird with gold-tipped wings. Robin smirked a bit and so I know I got it wrong but Rey said it was brilliant anyway.

But everything happens around us and we can't quite seem to join in properly. We're jigsaw pieces slotted into the wrong puzzle. Our edges are all wrong and I feel stuck. I can't work out what my brain wants because it's flipping my thoughts upside down and inside out.

Lissa puts Inigo down on a rug in the living room and tells us to make sure he doesn't fall out of a window or choke on a marble or crawl into the fire and all the other billion ways there are for a baby to hurt itself. Rey puts a barrier of cushions around him but he sneaks through and laughs and he speed-crawls off round the room like a tortoise that's been set on fire.

He's following his own little path and he zigzags and loops and slips behind the sofa and pops out at the other side and he's very pleased with himself. I watch him skitter and slide along the cold wooden floorboards and there will be so many babies after him and we will always be here to watch them.

It makes my heart sink down to my socks.

Chapter 18

That night I sit up in bed in our Light House tower and I try to stay awake. I need to see the fox because it will guide us into the wildlands. It will keep us safe just like it kept us safe when we were small and it was winter. And Rey won't leave without it. She keeps twisting her fingers and wondering how long it will take for the fox to lead us to our mother and I keep saying I don't know and I keep thinking how I don't care.

Our eyes itch and burn and stream and we sing quiet songs and we play Imagine but it's not enough. The darkness soothes us and we slide under. I dream of strange lands and of adventures that can't ever happen to me.

I jolt awake with a hummingbird heart. The others breathe a quiet sleep song and Rey is a tight ball of sharp elbows and folded knees.

I am ready to slip back into the warm and my dreams of boats through jungle rivers and balloon rides over deserts. But something stops me. I remember.

I look out of the frosted window.

The moon is bright tonight.

There is something out there.

I get up and I put on my boots. I don't even do them up and the laces swirl around my ankles like grass in the wind. I walk out of the quiet dark of the bedroom and down the silent stairs and out into the moonlit mist.

Something is slipping into the shadows. I see its shape shifting and my heart is wild but I am calm. I don't feel afraid. Not this time.

The thing slides from the darkness and I see the bright burned orange of its coat and the plume of its tail. It's the fox. Our fox. Perfectly drawn against the night like it's walked straight from the paper pages of one of Robin's books or stepped out of one of my stories with its inky paws. It slinks on to Rey's earth and I know it wants me to follow it so I walk on.

The fox stops and it looks at me with eyes that burn like fire through the mist.

Then the fox twists like running water and pads quietly away. I did something wrong. It is about to slip into the night and it will disappear and I wasn't quick enough and I've missed our chance and I've let Rey down and everything will be over before it even got started.

Then it turns and it stands by the fence and it is waiting and I can't believe it's true.

Our beginning.

Chapter 19

Everything is a rush.

I run back through the chill night air and I shake Rey from her soft dreams.

I saw where it went I say and I shake her again because she's curling back into a ball. *We have to go now. We have to go right now.* Rey is still dream-swamped and heavy and I grip her shoulders.

Rey, we have to follow. The fox is here. Waiting.

And at that word Rey shakes the sleep from her face and unfurls herself like a blooming flower. She springs up and we take the bags from under our bed and the smell of cheese is suddenly sharp.

Rey is glowing. It's like the moon outside has become part of her and she is luminescent and bright and brilliant. I want to hug her tight to me and hold this blazing new familiar Rey but we don't have time.

I take a look at Alice's face drowsy in the moonlight and I feel a bird of sorrow swoop in my chest because we are leaving and we are following something that might not even really exist and who knows where we're going and who knows if we'll ever be back because we're going to follow the threads of our story. I think about Robin waking me up to tell me about puffins and I think about Inigo's tiny feet ready for their first steps and I think about Lissa's hugs that wrap you up in velvet even when I don't think I want them.

All of a sudden I want to burrow under my soft quilt and pretend this was all a strange bright dream and I want to wake up tomorrow to porridge and mist and not knowing anything except here. I remember Marl telling us how the outside will swallow us whole.

But then Rey puts her hand in mine and her eyes don't show me my fear. She is standing tall and proud and brave and she is ready.

We tiptoe downstairs hand in hand. It's like we've practised and prepared for this moment and we dance careful steps that we both already know.

So we go.

Chapter 20

We go. We go out into the wild moonlit night. We go to where the fox is burning bright and waiting.

The cold snaps at my cheeks and I tighten my scarf even though the wool itches. I can't believe we're doing this. I can't believe that after eleven years of nothing but the Light House and the far horizon we are going to go out in the wildlands like I'd always dreamed and we're going to live under a never-ending sky and make our own story.

The fox sees us and its eyes flash but it doesn't move away. I move slowly to the gate but it's closed tight with a wrap of chain and a heavy padlock.

Marl has done a brilliant job of boarding us up and keeping us safe. There isn't a single gap in the wire fences that wrap around the bare garden. The posts are driven deep into the soft earth. Rey pushes against one with her tiny bird body and they keep pointing straight up to the stars. I try too but they're stuck fast.

Plan B I say and I rummage in my rucksack and carefully pull out the pair of extra-sharp scissors that I stole from Lissa's Dangerous Drawer, which is full of all the things we're not allowed to touch because we might lose a finger or cut our own hair or something. The blades gleam in the moonlight.

I crouch down in the earth and the damp cold slides straight through to my bones. I shiver but I snip and hack and twist at the chicken-wire fences. The metal doesn't want to give way and it pricks and tears at my skin and beads of blood pop through my flesh like tiny jewels. I lick them away and my mouth and the air are metal scented. I keep going even though everything burns and bites and after for ever and ever I have made a hole the size of two fists. It is low to the ground and the shadows cover it and I don't think Lissa will see.

OK, Fen? asks Rey and she is looking worried because my hands are smeared with sweat and blood. I have a horrible thought and it's that the smell of my blood will soar through the night air and the fox will turn and pounce on me like it leaped on the poor dead rabbit, but I swallow the idea down and I say *You bet.*

The fox blinks its beautiful eyes and then it turns in a movement like water rushing down a plughole and slinks under the hole I've just cut. Its tail flicks and the white tip disappears through the wire.

Quick I say and I say it with all the confidence that maybe I actually have tucked up inside.

Let's follow.

Fen, can't we go out through the gate? whispers Rey and she points in the other direction. I shake my head.

It's locked I say. *Come on, Rey, we have to go now, we have to go.*

I am desperate. I can't see the fox any more and Rey is being slow and careful and worried and this isn't the right time at all. Frustration is bubbling inside me and I want to shout at her and her quietness and her fear. But when you shout at Rey she disappears.

75

She is losing her moonlight glow. She is biting her lip. This is already too much for her and she's starting to turn back to the mouth of the house and I grab her hand and I pull her to me and I tell her that this is our chance. This is our chance to find her.

And Rey's glow flickers to life once again and we sink down and shuffle and crawl through the hole in the fence into the wildlands and she is right there with me all the way.

Chapter 21

The fox is waiting.

We emerge soilstained and scraped, with blood beading from our skin. Rey has a thousand leaves in her hair. We already look like we've been runaways for months. The word *runaways* pops and bursts in my head. That's what we are now. But we're not running away. We're running towards.

The fox cocks her perfect head and the stars shine in her fur. Her body twists and it flows through the air like liquid.

Come on I say and I grab Rey's hand and we follow the bright light of the fox's tail weaving in the mist.

I don't know what I was expecting from this side of the fence but I thought it might be more than just the same world. I thought maybe everything would suddenly tilt and shift and we'd lurch into something new and wondrous.

The ground is the same dark hardness. The sky is the same star-bright canopy. The mist is the same grey blanket. I can't see anything much except a crowd of trees bristling just ahead. I turn my head back for a moment and I see the house. I've never seen it from here before. Its edges blur in the night dark. A few windows glow warm orange. The lamp in the tower throws out light that brushes the ground with gold. I feel a tug somewhere in my belly. But I turn back and I see the white plume tail of the fox weaving and bobbing like it's floating away on an ocean. I keep my eyes on it and I don't look down or around because I cannot lose it. My ankles knock and bend on the uneven ground but I don't slow down and neither does Rey. We walk towards the trees and we follow the fox.

My muscles start to ache with effort and cold and my shoulders are rubbed raw by the straps of the backpack. We've probably packed too much but Rey wanted to be prepared. I haven't told Rey but part of me thinks that this is it. That we're walking towards our new home, our new lives, our new story. That the wildlands is where we belong and the wildlands is where we'll stay, no matter what. Even if we don't find what Rey is looking for.

As soon as we step into the forest my foot finds a hole. I have a moment where I know what will happen and I have a moment to put my arms out to catch the thud of my body as I whistle towards the earth and the shock of the ground ripples through my bones and the air is pressed out of my lungs and I can't move and I can't speak. Rey stops and she crouches down beside me in the silvery moonlight filtering through the waving branches and she says *Fen Fen Fen please be OK are you OK you have to be OK* and everything is coloured with her panic and my pain. I've lost all my air and I gasp and I try to spit my words out at the sky and Rey pinches my shoulder like I do sometimes to wake her up and the sharp bite of her fingers jolts my lungs back to life and I say *I'm OK Rey I'm OK don't worry* in a gasp of tumbled sounds that don't sound like me.

I scrabble to sit up and I look around and I search the still night and I push myself up from bruised knees and I scan a circle around us as far as my eyes can see but I know she's gone.

The fox has gone.

Chapter 22

I scan desperately for the smokeplume of tail or the glint of an eye or the flash of fired fur. But there's nothing. The night has swallowed her up and there is darkness lapping at our edges.

Which way? whispers Rey. *Which way now?*

I look up and down. The trees above have thickened into a ragged dark ceiling. The ground beneath my booted feet is exactly the same, like the world could be tipped up any way and it would all be the same. I take a deep breath. I nudge the earth with the toe of my boot and feel it shift and crumble. I strain my eyes to try to see something, anything, that might help us.

Let's just walk straight I say. *Just keep going straight ahead.*

OK says Rey because she trusts me.

We walk on through the cold and the wind and the thin streams of moonlight that silver the ground and it feels like hours and even though we have the path I am searching and searching for the burst of orange or the shape of something folding itself out of the night and coming to find us. I don't know why I'm so desperate to see her because it's Rey who believes, not me. But out here in the dark unfamiliar air I want something to believe in too. I want the fox to come back even though I've got what I wanted and we're in the wildlands now. I want it to come back for Rey, and I want it to come back for me. I want it to stay with us for a while. I want it to show us the way so I don't have to guess and keep trying to find the edges of a path in the black night.

Finally I get the lantern out of my backpack and I wind and wind and wind it until my aching arm is on fire and the orb inside throws out its light. There still isn't much to see. Trees cling to either side of us but we seem to be on a skinny path that winds and snakes between the trunks. There are forks and lines where the path wriggles away at different angles but there is a clear way forward. I think. I have to trust the wildlands. Because now there is no fox.

I try to taste the wind like Marl did and smell that odd musky scent that is all at once horrible and comfortingly familiar. I'm not sure if I think I can follow a smell instead of a fox but I try anyway because I've got nothing to lose. I sniff the brackish air and manage to swallow some spit and I cough and my eyes stream. I suddenly want to cry for real and the feeling swoops in and takes me by surprise but I am being ridiculous because we have only just left and I have made Rey a promise and I also would be really embarrassed if we slunk back now. But the thought of Lissa up and waiting for us with mugs of hot cocoa from her secret stash for poorly and sad children makes my heart do a funny dip.

Rey is silent even when I ask her if she's OK and she's sealed up tight and I don't know what she's thinking and it's all so different here. I feel like a kite thrown about on a fierce wind and no one is holding on to my string. I'm half excited to be flying and half terrified I'll disappear.

After a while we have to stop. We have no fox to follow and even though I want to trust that I know where I'm going the path is becoming thick with brambles that catch and tear at our clothes. The night is dark and hungry. My whole body aches and there are bruises seeping through my skin and bursting into blue stars.

I don't know how we'll ever sleep. I remember imagining sleeping out under a canopy of blinking stars, stretched on my back and Rey showing me cosmic patterns. But above us is just a batflap flutter of dark leaves and twisted branches. I whisper to Rey and I say *Are you OK? Are you too cold?* And she turns to cuddle in close to me and her body heat creeps into me and I put my arms around her and together we make a tangle that isn't quite warm but it's enough.

Let's play Imagine says Rey and I'm so glad she's talking. She feels like home. So I play.

Imagine she was waiting for us in the far-off wildlands all this time. She knew it was too dangerous for little babies but she knew we'd come back. She built a house and planted a garden and she tamed the wild things.

Imagine she was waiting for us to be big and strong enough to survive out here with her. Imagine if she sent a fox to tell us we were ready and imagine if this story is true.

Imagine.

Chapter 23

When we wake up in the pink morning foxlight I have no idea where we are. The pale light makes everything very different. It has pulled away the veil of the mist and I can start to see everything. The twists of trees and the scramble of leaves and dirt and tiny plants peering through the earth. The wildlands are a riot of pinks and yellows and blues and greens from the earth to the sky. It's brilliant.

I can see all the paths that dip and turn and wrap around us and for a moment I think of having to make the next choice but then Rey stretches beside me and she blinks and she looks and for a moment she looks so small and then she stands up and she looks at the whole world all around her and she is taller than I've ever seen her. She says *Fen, look at this* and she is touching the delicate fronds of a creeping green plant and she's full of wonder and it fills me too. The story from last night is still swirling in my brain and I look for the fox even though the light is melting into day.

Neither of us is really sure what to do. We eat some bread that's already starting to harden and curl and then a bit of the salty cheese and I feel a lurch because Zaki will be so sad. Cheese is a treat. But it makes us thirsty and I drink half a bottle of water until Rey puts her hand on my arm and tells me *Stop stop stop* and I realise I don't know where we'll get any more that's clean. I know there's a river somewhere out here but I'm not sure where and it could be full of anything and I remember Lissa telling me about rats peeing in river water and how it made people really sick and never to drink any water that wasn't boiled first and I thought that was such a weird thing to tell me because all our water comes from a tap and I'd never even seen a rat. But now I'm glad she told me and I don't want to drink rat pee and there might not even be rats out here but I don't want to risk it. But maybe we'll have to and maybe we'll just have to cope. I'm sure I can find fresh water here. I trust the wildlands.

The others will be having hot eggs and toast right now.

I say *We're going to find her, we're going to find our fox* and Rey nods and beams and then she looks around and there are a thousand different angles and directions and she turns back to me and I know she's waiting for an answer. There are paths that are trodden flat by animals or humans and they splinter and snake and cross and I don't know what to do. I thought maybe there would be a ping in my brain and I would just know what was right. Like when we play Imagine and I always know what comes next. I thought that each turn would feel familiar and like I'd studied it on a map a thousand times. But I'm just not sure now.

We just have to choose says Rey. *We have to choose and the fox will find us again. They don't really like the daylight. I read it in my book. But if we keep going the fox'll find us when she's ready. She has to, Mum sent her.*

Mum.

The word is funny. We never really talked about what we'd call her. But with that one word her image is suddenly sharpened in my mind without me having to try to imagine.

OK I say. *You choose then.*

Rey points down a path that is straight as an arrow. *This one* she says.

The path is flatter than the others. It has been tramped flat by feet or by paws and there are no vicious bramble teeth to fight through. It's a good choice.

Rey's face is eager and open and waiting and I nod and I say *OK let's go*.

And we walk together and I take Rey's hand and we watch for a flick of orange fur.

Chapter 24

It is cold but we are too sweaty and I start taking off layers and I think about a story I read once about a woman who was too cold but she thought she was too hot and she took off all her clothes and lay down in the snow and froze blue and heartstopped.

Rey keeps stopping to touch the plants and the curled frost-spangled flowers. She is taking in all the newness and the nature and the beauty through her fingertips and she marvels at the plants and she tells me they're astonishing and she strokes petals gently like they're pets or made of glass. The wildlands are already soaking into her and she's unfurling like one of the buds she's gently stroking. I touch the plants and feel the rough bark of trees against the smooth skin of my hands but there is no sparked moment of connection with the world I've longed for from my tiny window for all these years. I am just cold and a bit lost.

I am also impatient and my tummy rumbles because a mouthful of cheese and bread isn't enough. I am so hungry. I've never been this hungry because I've never had to be and I didn't think it would make me so moody and furious and my insides are electric with the need for food. We need to eat and I feel so stupid because I thought this would be easy and I didn't worry about things like running out of water and food. I just wanted to be here. I thought it would all just work out and somehow we'd step into a land filled with bright berry bushes and crystal clear waterfalls. I remember imagining us catching rabbits in traps and roasting fish on a fire and my cheeks flame.

Rey doesn't complain but I know she's hungry because I can sometimes catch the rumble of her tummy. She's too busy looking at everything and touching everything and pointing out tiny shoots struggling through the frosted ground and she doesn't notice her hunger one bit. I wish I could forget mine. The mist starts to fall around us. The mist is different here. It still swirls and lifts and curls but it isn't so furious and it isn't so thick. It's like a gentle swish of silk that rises and falls and sometimes it shows us everything and sometimes it hides the world. I keep looking for the burned ember of a fox sliding through the undergrowth but there is nothing.

We stop for lunch and I lay out the food parcels from my backpack. Side by side laid out in the huge air of the wildlands it looks like not very much at all and that's mostly because it's not very much at all and we have to split it between two. The light falls through the clouds above and patterns the bread like a painting.

The cheese is nearly all gone and I can't believe we had that much for breakfast. Back at the house I don't really think about how much there is to eat because even though I know Lissa is always a bit worried about stretching the pantry to feed us all when there's a new Foundling, she always manages and it's always delicious. Except for mouse-tail soup although right now I think I'd eat the whole bowl, grey gristle and all.

Right now there are still six slices of salty meat glowing like rubies and half a small loaf of bread that's hardening to a rock and a bag of dusty oats and raisins and sugar. That's it. We can't even cook the oats because we need clean water and a fire. I don't know if you can eat raw oats and it's exactly the kind of thing Robin or Lissa would know. I should have paid more attention and learned how to keep us alive. I have thought about the wildlands for my whole entire life but I never really thought about how I'd actually live out here. I feel my stomach twist with hunger and panic. I've never even really had to feel hungry before. Rey and I would always giggle and retch over how gristly and grey and lumpy the food was in the house but it filled our tummies and it was always there. Three times a day every day. Buttery toast in between if you were hungry. Cups of hot tea. Cakes on special days. Fudge sometimes just because.

Fen, how are we going to eat? asks Rey and I am too hungry and scared and I can't stop myself snapping like a wolf.

How am I supposed to know? I say and all my words are jagged and sharp and Rey shrinks back into the mists. *Why do I always have to have the answers?*

Rey stays quiet.

93

I take a deep breath.

Let's have something to eat now I say and I keep my voice calm and gentle. *And we can sort something out. We can't fix the problem if we're hungry, we can't think properly.*

I put slices of meat into bread and top it with the very last of the cheese. My tummy rumbles and my hands tremble and I want to eat it in one big bite but I'm also worried because I'm using way too much food but I just can't stop myself. When I close my eyes all I can see is a table laden with steaming bowls of soup and great chunks of bread and a huge trifle stuffed with jelly and custard and I want to disappear into my story.

Rey shakes her head when I give her a pink tongue of meat and crumbling yellow cheese wrapped in a hunk of bread and she only picks and nibbles and I feel my fury rising again.

Just eat it I say and I make the words short just like Marl does and Rey blinks and pushes the sweaty lump into her mouth and coughs and the whole thing lands on the soil with a wet thump.

94

We've hardly got any food and you've gone and spat it out I say but I don't really say it I shout it and it echoes off the trees. We've been out here for one night and I am stretched as tight as elastic and ready to snap. I take a deep breath.

Rey picks up the muddy sandwich and tries to brush the dirt off and I watch her gentle fingers picking soil from the bread and I feel so heartsick I want to cry. I grab her hand and I pull her to me and I whisper that I'm sorry and I hug her and I hold her very close and I tell her we'll find more food and we'll find everything we're looking for and I just have to find a way to make it all come true.

We'll find her Rey whispers back and I nod even though the mists are shifting again and I can't seem to find our mother's shape any more.

We sit back down on the damp earth and we share my sandwich.

Chapter 25

After the sandwiches we keep on the same path. The wildlands seem never-ending and there is no sign or smell of our fox. The story echoes in my mind and I want to speak it into the air and tell it over and over until the colours of the wildlands are painted with our truth. But Rey has scampered ahead and I would be talking to the trees.

I wipe my hand across my face and it's damp with sweat. My breath is ragged because all this walking is harder than I thought. I thump to the ground to retie my tattered laces, as if that will make a difference when the leather is falling apart around my ankles and I'm only really doing it so I can have a tiny break from walking. I crouch in the mud and I flick the laces round just like Lissa taught me. I'm pulling through the final loop when Rey turns towards me and her face changes when she sees me sitting in the mud with my damp face and broken boots. I can't read her expression but she turns away again before I can say a word.

Then she shouts and the sound echoes all around.

I stumble forward with my laces flapping and my boot loose but I don't notice even when my ankle twists and slides.

Fen, look! Rey is shouting again and she's pointing at the earth and she's grinning so wide that her face is like a broken sunbeam and she's hopping with excitement and her yellow hat is askew.

I see the shape stamped in the earth.

A footprint.

Wide and deep and ridged just like the footprints of someone wearing proper boots meant for walking in the wild. Or perhaps the stamp of a leaf or the shadow of an animal's paw or the print of stones once pressed into damp earth.

Someone was here she says. *Someone was here! We're going the right way. There are people out here.*

Rey's pale face is bright and everything she thought is true is true in her head. She kneels down and she pulls her sketchbook out of her pocket and she draws a picture of the footprint across two pages and she's so careful to make sure she puts in every ridge and whorl.

I don't say the words that are moving around my mouth like marbles. That the print is too big to belong to a woman. That the print might not even be a footprint at all. That it could have been frozen forever ago into untrodden earth on this unused path.

She's here I say. I bounce Rey's words back at her. *We'll find her.*

And we walk on, hand in hand.

Chapter 26

By the end of the day we have eaten even more of our food even though we've tried so hard to make it last and we are damp from the cold and the mist. I am shivering and Rey is rubbing her arms up and down to try to press heat into her flesh. We suck on sugar cubes for energy and I can just imagine Lissa telling us that our teeth will rot right out of our heads.

My teeth chatter but they don't fall out. The light is fading. The fox is nowhere to be seen but we haven't made it to the forest yet. There is still hope. I try to wrap myself in layers of it and I try to remember all the things I thought would be brilliant about being out here and being wild and free and being just us and no one else.

It's hard to think when your brain is starting to sparkle with frost inside your skull.

I blow out my breath and try to make smoke rings but my mouth is moving too much because of the cold and I can't feel my fingers any more. I wish I'd asked Lissa to knit me some gloves when I had the chance. She made some for Robin when he asked and she sewed little eyes on the top so he could shape his hands into roaring monsters whenever he wanted to make us laugh.

Rey and I need to make a fire.

If we can make a fire we can boil water and cook oats and keep warm and not freeze to solid ice. I'll be more sensible with the food when we have a fire. I'll cook leaves into soup and make porridge last for weeks. I feel a little fizz of excitement. This is how it should be.

The slight problem is that even though we have matches, neither of us knows how to make a flame leap to life and feed it so it stays bright and hungry. Lissa always lit the fires at home. They would scent the air with pine and smoke and something deeper and darker and it smelt like being wrapped up cosy on the sofa with a blanket and some toast dripping hotly with golden butter.

My mouth waters.

I try and remember what Lissa does. How she makes the flames dance. My mind strains and swirls and I am back in the warm house watching her lean over the sooty mouth of the fireplace and listening to her telling us all to settle down so she can tell us a story.

I pull together the threads of her movements. I hold the picture of the fireplace tight.

Rey, we have to get some sticks and some leaves but dry ones OK I say with a lot more confidence than I actually have.

Rey scampers along and she stops every so often to pick up something from the dark ground and I see her yellow woollen head dip down to the earth. We have stopped in the lowlands between two hills and they start to shift and change as the light fades. Their green sides turn black and they look like monsters crouching and ready to pounce. I swallow. Fire will give us protection.

I help Rey gather twigs and sticks that crumble at my touch. Rey hunts for moss because she's read it's good for burning but she can only find a few velvety handfuls. There are a lot of wet leaves and wet twigs but after a bit of searching and scrabbling around the base of trees we find what we need. I pile the little scraps into a heap and light a match with a fizz and a huff of smoke. When I touch it to the twigs they fizz and huff too but the tongues of flames lap and lick and then shrink. I grit my teeth. Rey takes a match and tries too but the same thing happens.

I remember Lissa kneeling by the fire, blowing it into life.

So I light a match and I try the same. At first there is nothing but hot wet smoke and the smell of charred soil. I keep breathing into the dark. Gentle air that slowly wakes the timid fire. And with a sudden rush and a spark the leaves and twigs curl into fire and the flames dance.

Rey and I actually dance with joy. We stamp and shout and wave our arms and we whoop and shout into the stardust sky.

You made fire Rey cries and she throws her arms around my waist and suddenly the forest and being away from everyone back at the house doesn't feel so strange. This is exactly how I wanted everything to be. The two of us, wild and alone.

We sit and warm our frozen hands by the fire and watch the smoke rise into the air. We haven't found much wood and so I know the deep orange heat won't last forever and I let it soak into my bones and the joy spreads through me like liquid. I get out the last few crumbling bits of bread and pierce them with a stick. We grill them over the flames and spray crumbs into the air as we giggle with the joy of dry toast. I boil a bit of our precious water and make steaming mugs of hot tea too. There's no milk to cut through the bitterness of the leaves but it still tastes sweet and delicious to me. I warm my hands on the metal cup and try to spot stars through the clouds above. Rey points to the North Star and a few others she knows from books but I can't tell them apart in the inky sea of diamond lights. Rey says the North Star is bright and bold and never changes but I still can't see it properly.

Rey gets out her little blue sketchbook and in the low glow of the flames she tries to fill the pages. After a while she stops and brings out a paperback and her fingers follow the words as they take her somewhere else. I keep looking for the orange flick of a fox but the blackness is deep and wrapped tight around the sky.

We start to doze off, leaning against each other still sitting up. Rey's book falls to the ground with a dry thump. My eyes are heavy and drooping and the world keeps disappearing.

Imagine … I whisper but I can't finish. I'm too tired. Every single fibre inside me is turning to treacle and stone. Even my hair feels tired. Somehow in the dark and the cold and the wildness I fall asleep.

Chapter 27

The next morning I jolt awake like lightning. I have a crawling feeling wriggling across the back of my neck. It feels like being watched. But when I look up and around there is no one but Rey and she is facing away from me and looking at something on the ground. I wonder if she's found more footprints. I stretch and my muscles grind against my bones. My eyes are gritty and my stomach is empty. The fire is grey and dead.

I go and see what Rey is looking at and she's staring in horror and it takes me a moment to follow her eyes to see what's happened.

There are scattered pages everywhere. They float across the trampled path and words dance in the breeze. The cover flaps uselessly like a twisted butterfly. Rey's paperback book is ruined. I spin around. One of our backpacks is lying on the ground but not where I left it. It's twisted and it gapes like a sagging mouth. Scattered all around it are the cloths we used to wrap up our food.

They're empty.

The final slender slices of meat. The tiny lump of dry cheese. The bag of oats. The chunk of bread. The sparkling sugar cubes. The wrinkly little raisins.

All gone.

Something wild and ravenous has taken them.

We have nothing left.

What happened? whispers Rey. *Who did this?*

Her voice is trembling because I think she knows and I know too.

I can see the needlepoint teeth marks and I can smell the strange musky scent caught in the air.

The fox I say. *The fox did this.*

Rey's face crumples.

It's not true she says. *The fox wouldn't do this. It was sent to find us, to protect us.*

The blood rushes in my ears and I put my head in my hands and I don't know what to do. I don't know what to say.

Rey looks very small. She's picking up the scraps of her storybook and putting them in her pockets, as if she can fit them all together later like a jigsaw puzzle. I want to do anything I can to make it better. But I can't. We are two tiny specks and we are lost in a furious wildland that's going to swallow us whole and we are cold and we are hungry and we have no food and we are alone.

We are alone.

And all the hopes inside me and inside Rey are flickering and stuttering like the smoke-filled fire last night. I don't know how to keep the truth and stories separate any more and I'm not sure which is which. I can't believe that the fox would do this. But then why wouldn't it do this? It's a wild thing. That's what they do. The thin golden thread that tied me to it and tied me to this place is frayed and starting to snap. I thought being out here would make me understand myself. But I don't understand the wild and I'm not sure who I am with or without it.

I am cold and icy and something inside me has changed. I search for the feeling and it's like running your tongue round your mouth to check your teeth and finding a tender hole where a tooth is suddenly missing. There was a tiny flame of hope and I didn't notice it until it was gone and now there is nothing but a hot shame that I ever let that flame spark at all. I feel like I've been tricked by my own brain and I am so stupid and small and angry.

We are alone.

Chapter 28

The rush of blood in my ears fades to a trickle and I can hear myself think and I know what to do.

I think we should go back I say to Rey. *It's not going to work. It was an adventure but it's over now. But we can go back and have tea and toast and play Imagine by the fire and you can garden again and I can … well it doesn't matter what I do.*

As I say the words tea and toast and fire I can almost taste them and feel them and I am suddenly a little bit warm and a little bit full. It makes me sure that it's the right thing to do. I think of the dark shaping and twisting itself into the night yesterday and I feel a niggle of something but I squash it down. It's not enough. We have to go back.

Rey looks at me like I have turned into a turnip.

She shakes her head so fiercely that I worry it will roll off and away down the valley.

We had tea and toast last night and it was magic. We can't go back, Fen she says and for a moment I think she might say what I'm thinking, which is that we're a bit lost and going back is about as easy as going on. But she doesn't. She stands with her hands on her hips and she's a perfect outline cut sharp against the morning light and she is sure and she looks like part of this world.

We can't go back. Not yet. Please. It's not enough. Not yet.

She looks like she wants to say something else but she stops and lets her voice fade away and her words are fierce and perfectly shaped and she throws them out like smooth pebbles across a river. They shatter something inside me. She looks so solid and true as she stands with the wind pulling her hair through its fingers like silk. Like she belongs.

I am so tired and so hungry and I don't think for one single second that I have enough inside me to carry on. My grip on our story is slipping. But Rey won't go back. I know that if I made her, if I shouted and screamed and dragged her, or if I walked off, she would follow me. But even though she's been blue with cold and furious with hunger, this is the most alive I have ever seen Rey. She's blossoming and unfurling in the mist and among the flowers. There is something here that's taking root in her and she is growing and I can't rip her away and take her back and watch her fade again.

OK I say. *OK. We'll go on.*

We gather the tattered backpack and we walk on down the path we've chosen. Rey looks at tree bark and I try to find something of myself in the shapes of the branches.

Chapter 29

My feet are blistering in my boots. I can feel the rub of my skin against leather. I am rapidly becoming very grumpy. We have had nothing to eat for breakfast because we have nothing to eat for breakfast, so we have little sips of water as we walk and we play Imagine except with food.

Imagine fat rashers of bacon.

Imagine a big hot chocolate.

Imagine fried eggs with gooey yolks that spread like a sunset.

Rey pulls a face because she likes weird hard yolks that crumble in your mouth.

Imagine toast with salty butter.

Imagine beans and mushrooms whispers Rey and she's joining in just a bit.

I pull a face because mushrooms are like eating

grey rubber and Robin once told me they grow in dung.

Imagine strawberry jam and raspberry jam and apricot jam and blackberry jam.

Imagine vanilla sponge with fresh cream and strawberries.

Imagine cheese on toast fried in a pan and crispy all over.

We keep going and my legs burn and my blisters rub and we both trip and scrape our hands and graze our bruised knees and all around us the world is suddenly wild and cruel and strange and I wish we'd turned back because I think I might have been wrong about all of this. It's not how I imagined. It's not the story I told myself.

But we keep going and by the time we've planned a breakfast that would make a table collapse, the mists are fading and the light is growing.

We step out of the shadows and into the sun.

Chapter 30

We are at the top of a hill that rolls down into a valley. The whole world is spread out in front of us.

The sun blooms into the folds of the land and I feel free and the fury and worry from the morning seem to evaporate in the air. These wildlands are astonishing. There is so much to see and my eyes can't quite take it all in because they have never seen more than the faraway horizon from the house and that is always grey and ghostly. There is so much colour here. The bare ground is spongy and sprigged with grass. Some of it sticks straight up in great plumes but much more is flat and slicked to the earth. The land is brown and green and golden and blue and bronze and it rises and falls like a patchwork sea draping itself over mountains and flowing down into valleys. Rey dances through the air and the fox's betrayal evaporates in the sunlight as she jigs with delight. Every so often she stops to write something and I look around us and try to take it all in and sometimes I borrow a bit of paper and try to draw what I see.

Dark craggy peaks of mountains tipped with snow and the green and gold curve of hills and slopes that roll towards the ground and then rush to meet the sky. Trees with bare branches scratching the air and trees with thick forest coats. A thousand different grasses that spike sharply and melt to velvet. The whole sky stretched over us like a blazing dome.

There are plants and grasses that twist and tumble together like great balls of green wool. Bright leaves are scattered on the ground and there are tiny tight flower buds waiting for enough warmth. There is a blue twist of river that loops its way towards us and away from us and disappears. It hisses as the water is pulled along at a speed that makes its surface blur. In the distance I can see the pointed teeth of more mountains or maybe hills and I can see the dark fur of dense trees pressed against the far horizon.

There is so much space. There is so much choice.

I can see flattened paths crossing and snaking and turning and disappearing. The air is quiet and the only flickers of movement are the sway of grass and the shivering of tree branches in the wind.

Even if there is someone, anyone, out here there is so much space that we would never find them through all the mountains and hills and forests and winding paths. I imagine that person living tucked away in the fold of a valley or the peak of a mountain, hidden from the world. Catching rabbits in traps and cooking spitting meat over a fire that smokes up to the starlit sky. Reading the same old books in the fading moonlight and singing the same lines of songs over and over until they're worn smooth as glass in her throat. Alone. And wild.

I take Rey's hand and together we run down the hill and it's like we're flying. The wind rushes by and the world rushes by and I feel free and I feel alive and all the worry and the hunger and stress are blown out of me by the cold and the beauty.

When we get to the valley below I immediately go to the river and I put my hands into its icy flow. The water runs over my skin and it burns and bites with cold but it feels like silk. After a while the burning stops and my hands are blue and my bones stiff with ice but it soothes my scraped hands and it feels delicious.

I wish we'd come in summer and then we could swim I say to Rey and she looks baffled but I imagine sinking beneath the cool surface and washing away the blood and dirt and soil and my skin being sparkling new. The wildlands are shifting and changing into what I wanted and hoped and knew that they would be. Maybe we'll still be here in the summer and we'll strip off our winter clothes and pour our milkwhite bodies into the bonecold depths. I imagine it and for a flash there is someone else there, holding out fluffy towels and giving us steaming cups of tea and laughing when we pretend to be fish blowing bubbles in the blue water.

But now the wild feels so empty. Just us. Two girls and two backpacks under a misty sky in the heart of the wild. I call out just to hear the sound of a human and I shout

Hello

into the mists and the sound bounces off the hills and back at me.

Hello-hello-hello

I turn because it sounds like someone is there, right beside me and yet very far away. But there's no one and it's my lonely echo.

Chapter 31

Playing Imagine with food is quite fun for a while but it doesn't fill you up even though I can actually taste the salt and the sugar on my tongue. My mouth waters.

I'm so hungry I whisper to Rey like it's a secret. She is kneeling down and writing something in her notebook and she doesn't seem to hear me even though the world is silent.

There are so many new things here she says and she is full of wonder and petals. *I never thought I'd see them all.*

We're starving to death in the middle of a valley and no one knows we're here, but Rey is enjoying the flowers. That's all right then.

We need to eat I say more loudly.

We can forage something says Rey dreamily. *I bet the*

wilders did that. How else would they have survived? I bet there's delicious food right beneath our feet. We just have to look.

I love Rey and she is my sister and I would die for her, but she is bonkers. She believes in the wilders with every ounce of her skinny self and she thinks that their supposed existence means we won't die of malnutrition. For just a moment I wish I could be more like Rey. That I could believe and hold on to hope no matter what. But I'm not. I'm realistic.

Food? Here? I throw out my arm so it sweeps through the valley with its scrubby grasses and its pops of flowers. There are no bright berry bushes or laden apple trees like I imagined. *What are we going to have? Soil soup?*

But Rey has wandered off towards a spiky clump of green shoots.

I sit down and I watch her open her notebook and look at its pages and then look at different clumps of plants that all look the same. She sticks her careful fingers into leafy bushes and sprouts of grasses and she works her way through the belly of the valley.

She comes back with her hands cupped together in front of her like she's carrying glass.

Look she whispers. *Look.* She is marvelling at what she's holding out as if it's the most precious treasure in all the world and I look and I don't know what I was expecting but it was not this.

In her hands are little egg-shaped lumps wrapped in green leaves. There are maybe fifteen of them and they look disgusting. I shrink back and Rey looks offended.

They're hazelnuts she says and she splits open the egg and out pops a little brown nut. She grins and throws the nut into her mouth and chews it so loudly that her teeth are probably going to crack and splinter.

Delicious she says and she pops another one and I feel a bit sick but also a lot hungry.

Are they safe? I say but I don't actually really care. At this stage I'd eat a toxic rat just to have the weight of something in my stomach.

Rey nods and I grab one from her hand and split the strange eggy outer layer. I stuff the nut into my mouth and chew and chew and it's not the nicest thing I've ever eaten but it's not the worst either. It's dry and also somehow a bit greasy and a tiny bit sweet but there's a strange tangy aftertaste.

How did you know? I say as Rey spreads the nuts between us and we sit down and picnic like we're on a day trip and have jam sandwiches and lemonade.

Read it somewhere. Wrote it down she says *and I described the plant just in case. Maybe you could draw it now?* She's shy and pleased and pink. She is learning how to be wild and how to live here and I am filled with pride but I'm a little bit jealous too because this isn't how I thought it would be and the wildlands are crueller and more brutal than I ever could have imagined. I thought they'd wrap around me and I'd sink into them like a second skin but they just don't fit me. I rub my blisters and eat another hazelnut.

You're brilliant I say when I've finished chewing and I mean it because I push down the little flame of jealousy until it splutters and hisses and dies. We feast on the handful of hazelnuts and it's not very much but it's enough for now. I sketch the hazelnuts and the plants for Rey and she gives me a hug and labels them in her careful handwriting.

122

We should be getting on with the journey but there is a weak pool of sunlight filling the dip between the hills and I can almost imagine it's warm. Rey's hazelnuts have filled my belly and I feel a rush of love towards her and so I start the story I know she wants.

Imagine she walked this walk every single day and imagine she foraged for hazelnuts and she made them into biscuits and cookies and all the wilders loved her because of that and because she was brilliant I say and Rey stops poking through the soil and looks up. She grins at me and her whole face breaks open with joy.

Imagine she grew strange plants and she stewed them all up to make big vats of steaming soup that cured colds and headaches just like that I say and I click my fingers. *Imagine all this wildland was hers and she was bringing it back to life and every flower and every petal and every blade of grass is here because she grew it and she loved it.*

Rey curls close to me and she says *This is perfect, isn't it* and so instead of walking we play Imagine until the sunlight sinks back into the clouds and darkness is falling and we haven't gone anywhere at all but we're close to something.

When night arrives there isn't enough kindling for a fire but we curl up close together and we share each other's warmth. When Rey yawns her breath clouds around us and there is frost spangling the earth in the fading light. We are wound round each other and as the stars prick and peep in the sky it feels like a beginning.

I wake with a jolt in the fading dark of morning. My legs are pins and needles and my fingertips are blue but that's not what's woken me. I can hear something.

Then I see it.

There is a movement. A twist of something shadowlike and quick as smoke racing through the black and up the hill. A tiny firespark of sinew and fur glowing just for a moment in the foxlight.

And I feel that wild pull of golden thread between us.

I shake Rey's shoulder, gently at first and then harder and harder until her eyes fly open and she sees it too.

Chapter 32

I keep my eyes trained on the fox. It streaks in and out of thick grass and keeps racing up the side of the hill. It doesn't look back but it threads its way through the landscape, showing us the perfect path up and out of the valley.

It's hard work to climb the hill but we don't complain and we don't say a word. We keep pushing forward and thorns tear my skin and branches whip my cheeks and there is nothing ahead of us except never-ending hillside and my breath is getting lost in my chest.

Then all of a sudden there is land below us and there is sky stretched out around us.

We've made it to the top of the hill.

We are on top of the world.

I feel like we are queens and conquerors and below is all our brilliant, beautiful land.

I feel free.

We can see the tufts of dark forests and the swish of the next bit of river and the folds of the land stitched to peaks and mountains and hills. So much space and light and dark and air. I shout into the cold and my voice fills the space around us. I whoop and holler and clap and the land roars back. Joy spangles up my spine.

And when we step over the brow of the hill I see it. Hidden from sight, nestled away in a dip of the hillside.

Chapter 33

A house.

That fiery shadow led us here. I know it did. The fox led us here.

I can't believe I wanted to go back to the Light House. I can't believe I nearly gave up. I can't believe I thought Marl was wrong and that no one had ever lived out here and that it was all a myth and a story. I nearly gave up on the wildlands and our story and our beginning and everything that will make us understand who we are. And now we've found a house and now we can start to live out here properly. I feel giddy with excitement and I throw my arms around Rey and there's a spark of joy and hope that zips between us like magic and we whirl around and hold each other and whoop into the sky.

It's not exactly a proper house. It's more like the

pantry store back at the faraway Light House. It's not big enough to be an actual house I don't think. A little rectangle with a sharply sloping roof and walls freckled with stones. Two tiny windows and a little chimney. A small solar lamp that flares and flickers every so often and beams out into the haze. A wooden front door. There is a strange mark carved right into the chalky stone over it but I don't get a moment to look at it because Rey is already running towards the door and I can't wait either.

I run forward with Rey by my side. I knock on the door because what if there's someone here, and then my heart skitters because what if there's someone here? Rey says it as I bump my fist against the wood.

What if this is her house? she asks and her eyes are shining bright. *What if the fox brought us to her house, just like I said?*

I don't know how to answer and what if there is someone here who can tell us who our mother is and might even be our mother, and that thought stops my fist dead. The thump echoes inside and I can only hear emptiness.

128

I try the door and I'm absolutely expecting it to be locked because none of this has been easy, but it swings back on hinges that screech like the cry of the rabbit and I fall backwards with the force of it. I land on top of Rey and I worry for a moment that I've squashed her flat but she gets up and doesn't even brush off her knees because she's too busy darting through the dark jaws of the house and I know she's hoping that our mother will be waiting for us and I'm not sure what I'm hoping for.

I follow her inside.

Chapter 34

The house is empty. I know instantly. There is no other heartbeat in here.

It doesn't look like anyone has been here for a very long time.

Inside it's dark and it smells like damp. There is daylight outside but the windows inside are tiny and thick with dirt. It takes a moment for my eyes to learn to peer through the gloom. The room reveals itself slowly. It might be the most beautiful thing I've ever seen.

There is a round wooden table with two stubby wax-dripped candles in the middle and a chair with a leg that's splintered and been carefully mended. Next to it is a set of shelves and there are books and tins and papers and all the signs of a life. There is a spindly ladder that stretches up to a kind of balcony and on it

I can see the legs of a bed and the fold of a soft blanket. There is the sooty mouth of a fireplace and a small pile of logs stacked neatly and a woven basket stuffed with twigs waiting to be turned into warmth. There are silver pots and pans strung up like Christmas decorations on the chimney breast. There is a rusty sink with a tap that glows like a jewel. A huge pair of gardening gloves hang by the back door, soil stitched into their seams.

My disappointment dissolves but a little lump of it lodges somewhere deep inside me and I can feel it nudging and wriggling but I can't listen. I am so excited about what I can see that I can barely breathe.

Water.

Heat.

Maybe even food.

I go to the shelves and I start rifling through. Tins of peaches. Tin of beans. Tins of potatoes. Tins of trifle. I didn't even know you could get trifle in a tin. It's like the very best Found Day ever. There are grimy bags of sugar and oats too and I am already working out how much we'll be able to eat now and how much we'll be able to carry. My tummy rolls and clenches and I nearly stuff a handful of sugar into my mouth right then and there but I wait because I want to feed Rey too and she's scampered off somewhere in the gloom.

I run the tap and the water is crystal clear and I'm so thirsty I think I would have drunk it if it was brown and smelt like frogs. I gulp right from the tap and I guzzle and swallow and drink until my tummy feels fat and stretched like a drum and then I fill our bottle and make sure Rey has as much as she needs. She's running her fingers along the spines of books and she opens one and it coughs dust. She drinks wildly but she keeps her eyes on the curled pages.

Rey I cry when I find a little bar of foil-wrapped chocolate and I break it in half and I give her six milky brown squares and stuff the rest in my mouth. It melts on my tongue and it is the best thing I have ever tasted in my whole life. The sugar fizzes through me and I am wild with excitement and happiness and I hug Rey and I dance around the tiny room and I can't believe we've made it somewhere and we have chocolate and food and firewood and water. Rey giggles and her mouth is full of chocolate.

I dart around the room and I look in the tiny wooden cupboards that are full of startled spiders and dust and strange brown packets of what look like the seeds Rey likes to plant in her garden. I clamber up the ladder and see the bed and a bucket next to it and I wonder what the bucket is for and then I realise and say *Gross* even though we've been weeing in bushes for two days. I scuttle back down the ladder and I open more drawers and I find matches and four firelighters and a pen dribbling black ink and I've never been in a toy shop or a sweet shop but I think this is better.

I open one more rattly drawer and inside is a single scarf. It's knitted but with tiny little stitches, not the big loopy ones Lissa uses when she makes us stuff. It looks like a cobweb and I'm almost afraid to touch it. When I do it brushes my fingertips like a tiny breath and I pick it up and hold it up to the dim light. It is made of moonlight. I wrap it around myself even though it is probably full of a thousand furious spiders and those mites that like to burrow into your ears and nest in your brain. Robin told me about them once and I didn't speak to him for four days. I hold the scarf tight around my body and I wonder who it belonged to and instead of wondering aloud to Rey I fold up the scarf and put it in my pocket where it curls like a sparkling secret.

Rey is going much more slowly. She's still looking through the books and the papers and I can't believe she has the patience to stop and read and thumb through scraggly notes and dusty pages and funny hand-drawn inky lines spidering their way across yellowing paper, but she doesn't look up even when I tell her about the tinned trifle.

We try to light a fire in the filthy grate. I was already dirty and my skin was stained with blood and mud and grass and bruises, but now I am so raggedy that when I see my reflection in one of the pans I jump backwards and trip over a chair. I am wild-haired and the whites of my eyes glow bright in my soot-dusted face. I look like something from the pages of a story from long ago and drawn with ashy charcoal lines.

Lissa would say I should stick my head under the tap and wash the wildness from my hair but I don't want to and so I don't.

Lighting the fire is extremely difficult and I swear even though Lissa would boot me into the moon for saying words like that but she's not here to hear me and Rey doesn't mind. She giggles and then she tries to stack the logs in a pyramid but they collapse and shower us with splintery air. They have made a nice little pile so I fling a lit match into the mess and it hisses and smokes and the flame disappears in a split second.

I want to scream. This was meant to be easier. We have all the right things. We're not out in the howling wildlands in the mist and the drizzle and even then I managed it once. We have firelighters and a fat box of matches and a house and even chocolate and we belong here. And I still can't do it.

Rey has wandered away and back to the shelves as if she'll magically find a fire hidden among the crisp pages of old books. She sits down cross-legged and sticks her nose in a book and doesn't look up even when I swear again and it's a much worse word than before.

I light a match and I blow on the logs and they cough and blow back a mouthful of ash into my face. Grey specks burn my eyes and I scream with frustration and I hate this stupid fireplace. The buzz of the chocolate and the house and the scarf has worn off. I'm so hungry that I think we'll just eat cold beans and be cold until we leave and how bad can it really be if there's ice in your boots and tingling along your eyelashes?

I close my eyes and I try to remember how Lissa made the logs sit together in a neat pyramid. I try to remember what she said. The image of the flames as tiny animals sparks something. A memory. Her words float into my head.

Every living thing needs space and air and food. And I think fires are alive, look at the way it waves hello.

Air! I say as if it was obvious all along. *Of course. It needs to breathe. It just needs some space to breathe.*

I stack some small logs and then a few twigs from the woven basket. I make sure there are gaps between them and then I throw a firelighter into the very middle of the pile. I strike the match with a scrape and a fizz and touch it to the firelighter and then throw it into the logs. They gulp it down.

The flames dance and flicker and stretch like they're just waking up. They curl around the wood and they twist together and the heat begins to seep into our bones. I forget about my rumbling belly and my aching body and I sit with Rey on a raggedy rug that's patched and sewn together and falling apart and we watch the fire as it brings us back to life.

Chapter 35

We need to eat and we choose a tin of beans because they'll be quick and delicious and I know how to cook them. First I have to work out the tin opener because I've never used one before and all the tins we have at the Light House have little rings you can pull. I have to clamp the circular metal jaws on to the outside of the tin and turn a handle round and round. But it doesn't work. The tin opener just digs its teeth in and refuses to move and I twist and pull and grunt and shout but the beans stay hidden away and I am so hungry and so furious.

Rey takes the tin from me but she can't twist the metal in the right way either and her careful fingers glow red with effort. I snatch it back without meaning to snatch and I stare at it without doing anything for about a minute and I'm about to give up and bash it against the stone hearth of the fireplace when my hands make a sudden swift movement and the tin lid peels back and there are bright orange beans nestled inside like jewels. The very best treasure.

I make the beans. There is a funny little tripod thing that you can put over the fire and a pan sits perfectly on top of it. I pour the beans in and they start bubbling almost immediately. The smell makes my mouth water and I nearly dribble but I don't even care. The air is full of sugar and salt and tomatoes. I've never been so hungry in my whole life and I can't wait any longer. I give the beans a quick stir with a cracked wooden spoon and I lift the pan off the heat and put it between us. I don't even bother getting bowls. We eat straight from the pan using the big wooden stirring spoon and the beans are boiling hot on the outside and still icy in the middle but it doesn't matter one single bit because this is the best food I have ever eaten. I am not being careful at all and I'm getting bean juice all down myself and I think how Lissa would be horrified because bean juice stains and then I look at my filthy raggedy jumper and laugh through a mouthful of food. A single bean falls into my lap and I pick it off and eat it anyway. Rey is streaked orange. We don't care. We keep stuffing spoonful after spoonful of soft beans into our mouths until our bellies start to ache. I scrape out the pan with my hands and lick the sweet sauce from my black-etched fingers and this might be the best meal I've ever eaten. It is definitely better than a cold handful of foraged hazelnuts but I don't say that because I don't want Rey to think it wasn't amazing to find food in all that wild.

Afterwards we lie on our backs on the woven rug and stare up at the cobwebs glittering in the flame light. Anything feels possible with a full belly and a roaring fire.

Do you think this is her house … says Rey and her words trail off and fly up the chimney with the firesmoke.

I don't think so I say. But as I look around I wonder. The books. The scarf.

When I think about her she's exactly that. A thought, a misty shape in my mind that I can pull and twist and play with like clay. She's what I make her,

140

tucked away as a shadow in our stories. But now there's a new thought that's growing and sharpening its edges. A thought that's spinning and shining and weaving itself like the gossamer threads of a glittering scarf. That she's out there. That she's the answer. That she is the pull I've always felt. She is the thread that ties me to this world. That she will help me understand it. That she will help me understand myself. That she's real.

You know says Rey and she goes quiet for so long that I think maybe she's fallen asleep and then she starts again.

You know, I think the fox did it on purpose. Ate our food.

Why would it do that? I say and I'm thinking of the wild land and wild animals and how it's all so far beyond anything I thought I could understand.

To get us here. To make us keep going so we'd find food and shelter. To set us on the right path. The path that will find her.

I raise my eyebrows and feel them disappear into my tangled hair but Rey doesn't need me to answer.

She gets up and I don't know how she can bear to move. I am so full and warm and sleepy. She's prowling round the bookshelves again. I close my eyes and listen to the crackle of the fire and the whisper of paper pages.

Chapter 36

I hear a thump and I open my eyes. I have fallen asleep by the fire and it's hard to pull myself from my delicious sleep. Being inside is so much better than I remember.

Rey is standing by the bookshelf. There's a book splayed on the floor and she's staring at a piece of paper. It's covered in black lines but I can't see much more than that. I open my mouth but Rey takes the piece of spider-tracked paper and she goes outside.

Rey I shout croakily into the musty air and I choke a little on the dust and the damp. I don't want to go outside and I don't want to leave this perfect little space. But she doesn't answer so I burst into the mellow light outside.

Rey is staring up at the front door. Or above it. In her hands is the little scrap of paper.

Look she whispers. Above the door is the carved picture I saw on the way in. I don't really understand it. It's a loop that wriggles and stretches and then splinters into tiny flecks.

Yeah, what is that? I say and I don't expect Rey to know but she says slowly like a river stumbling over stones

I

think it's

a hazelnut

and she's so clever I want to hug her and I do and she grins and then she points to the paper and I look at it too.

And the whole world here opens up.

It's a map.

Chapter 37

It's not an ordinary sort of map because that would make life too easy and that's never been how it is for us.

But the reason Rey ran outside with the delicate onion skin of ink and paper is because dotted all along the hand-drawn paths and valleys and mountains and peaks and hills and rivers are tiny little houses. The tiny houses are evenly spaced like someone has taken a ruler and measured perfectly, even though the rest of the map is so loopy and trembling. They stretch from end to end until the paper stops.

Inside the belly of each house is a different symbol.

Rey's finger points to a dip beneath a hill and there is a little ink house nestled at its bottom. Inside is the same hazelnut symbol. We are right in the middle of the map and scattered behind us are tiny houses and there are more in front. I can see the scribble of the forest we fought through and ahead there is the swish of a river and the crags of mountains spiked in ink.

We are in the map and we are on the map and maybe we're not so alone.

Rey draws a path with her fingers, walking them along to each house. The ink is blooming and faded and cracked but we try to work out what each tiny symbol might be.

A flower

A fish

A hazelnut

A seed

A bird

A fox

A fox a fox a fox.

Bat eared and pointy nosed, three tiny triangles scribbled in a tiny house far away from this one.

It's where she'll be Rey says and her confidence shines like a pearl. *It has to be.*

An image flashes in my mind and it's a tall woman with Rey's autumn curls and my dark eyes and she's opening a door and looking down at us. I let the idea of our mother grow inside me like a seed. The seed wriggles and a tiny green shoot peeps through.

Let's make a plan I say and we go back inside.

Chapter 38

Tomorrow, we'll go tomorrow I say. *We'll pack up as much as we can from here, maybe everything and we'll go to the flower house. It's the next closest.*

Not everything says Rey and she looks up from *A Field Guide to Mushrooms*.

I stare at her.

Someone else might want it she says. *Wilders. We don't need it all.*

Rey goes back to the pages of muddy-capped mushrooms and I imagine the shifting tides of people hidden in the wildlands and moving from house to house and fading in and out of the mist. I think of the layer of dust on the kitchen table and the musty smell of the bed blankets and the cracked yellow pages of the books on the shelves. I think of the neatly stacked firewood and gunmetal shine of tins and tins of food.

148

I think of Marl saying everyone was gone. I think of staring out of the windows of this house on the hill and seeing nothing but the shifting light and empty skies. I think of that maybe-footprint in the mud and how long something like that might last in the frozen ground.

I think of the very last house on the map and the shadow of our mother sharpening into real edges and the soft feel of her arms wrapped around us and how she'd say *My babies my babies you found me.* I think of my stories being true.

Yes I say *you're right. Let's leave something for the other people.*

Chapter 39

That night Rey is shining bright. We eat the tin of trifle and it's somehow both delicious and disgusting. I'm better at using the tin opener this time and the lid peels back like magic.

We sit by the fire and eat food and do nothing else but talk and laugh and tell stories about our mother. It is perfect. I finger the cobwebs of the scarf in my pocket and I feel a little starburst of guilt because I've kept this a secret from Rey, and so in the warm glow of the fireflames I show her and for a moment her face is still and quiet and I wonder if she'll hate that I kept it from her but then she smiles. She holds it up and the fireglow makes it glittering and luminous and she runs it through her hands like water and I feel a tiny stab of something deep inside and I want to snatch it back because even though I'm spinning a

150

story from words and nothing, it feels like the scarf is all I have of her and I don't want to share. But Rey rubs it against her face and then wraps it around both of us because she is kind and good and I pull her close to me and I carry on sharing the story.

Imagine. Imagine she went on a journey just like ours. Imagine she was searching for a very special fox. A fox who knew a secret that she had to discover. A fox who lived at the very edge of the world under this wild sky. She went from house to house and she marked each one with something she saw there. She was here once and she made this rug from old scraps and she cooked food in this very pot. She left this scarf so that we'd know she was here.

When she found the fox in that very last house she carved its face and she learned its secret. But she had to keep that secret safe. So she left us and in return the foxes kept us safe. She knew she could send for us when we were ready to keep the secret safe too. So she stayed in that house at the very edge of the world and one day she knew it was time. She sent a single firebright fox into the misty night. And then she waited. She waited for us.

I stop saying *Imagine* and I start to make the story true. I keep saying it and each time I see her a little more clearly and she's a sharp outline in the mists and the fog and she's waiting for us at the very edge of the world. I make it true for Rey, but when I look over she's asleep.

Chapter 40

I wake up and for a moment I am back in the Light House and everything is how it always was.

I blink in the morning light and I wonder why it's so quiet and why Zaki hasn't shoved a toy car up my nose and why the air doesn't smell like eggs and porridge.

Then I see the tiny window and the world outside and the sloping roof and the golden needles of straw poking through the mattress and I remember. I clamber down the ladder and leave Rey in a huffing little ball under the blanket.

I feel electric after a full night of sleep with no prickling eyes watching me and no sky open above me and no wind charging through my bones. I am full of energy and excitement and the thought of maps and mothers and freedom and wildness. The fire is still glowing so I throw one more log on to keep us toasty while I make breakfast and pack our bags. I do as Rey said and I don't pack everything and I don't think we could carry it all anyway. I pick tins that sound like they might be tasty. Mince and beans and peaches in sticky syrup and trifle and chicken soup and spaghetti and tuna. Rey tries to add a handful of firelighters and I put my hand out because living wild and free shouldn't mean using things like firelighters and we need to get better at lighting fires without them. But Rey insists and Rey hardly ever insists so I let her even though my bag is really heavy now because I've put all the fire stuff and the heavy food into my backpack and I just leave Rey with some water and some light packets of crumbly oatcakes and a few bars of white-bloomed chocolate. I make sure I put some of that in my bag too though, just in case an animal snaffles one of our bags. Chocolate feels very important right now and probably always.

I fold the map carefully and put it in my pocket. I go outside and the sky is heavy. I empty the bucket in a bush and rinse it under an outdoor tap that sticks out like a knife from the stone side of the house. The water is freezing cold and my hands turn from purple to blue to white like a kaleidoscope of skin.

I go inside and warm my hands next to the flames and then I make porridge over the fire. I have to use water and not the creamy milk that Lissa gives us because she says it makes our bones strong and our teeth white. It doesn't smell quite as good as when I cook it in the Light House. I eat mine quietly and quickly and it's not too bad. It's better than nothing. I hope Rey likes it and I carry her bowl up the ladder very carefully so she can have breakfast in bed.

I shake Rey softly by the shoulder and whisper her name. Even though I'm gentle she wakes with a start and blinks in the light like a startled creature disturbed in its nest. I give her the bowl and she snaffles it down in four hot gulps and grins.

Like home she whispers and I don't know what to say so I just take her bowl back and wash it up before the porridge hardens and turns into shards that could cut your fingers right off.

Rey slides down the ladder without letting her feet even touch the rungs and lands lightly on her bare feet. She's alive with adventure.

I made the bed she says. *I tried to make it look cosy and clean.*

I give her her backpack and she looks inside and back at me.

I've got the heavy stuff I say and Rey looks cross and she opens her mouth but I take out the map and say *Let's get going or we won't find the next house by sunset.*

She closes her mouth and fiddles with the laces of her boots as she pulls them on.

Ready? I say and she nods.

I look around. I love this place already somehow. Last night was perfect. Now it doesn't look like we've been here at all. We haven't changed a thing except for some gaps in the dusty shelves. And the cobwebbed scarf that is nestled softly in my pocket.

Chapter 41

The map isn't the clearest thing I've ever looked at because the world doesn't really look like scribbly black lines and it definitely doesn't look like these scribbly black lines that could have been drawn a thousand years ago. I wonder if the whole landscape has shifted and changed like the mist and actually the whole map is totally wrong because I can't see anything that matches even when I spin and turn and strain my eyes to the horizon. We have a very small argument about which way to go and do quite a lot of holding the paper upside down and turning it round and looking for trees that look like stacked triangles.

It's towards the hill over there I say firmly and Rey shakes her head and points at a path in the opposite direction. I turn the map upside down again and then try and turn my head upside down.

It could be either way really. I thought having a map would fix our wandering but it's not helping at all. I've never had to read a map before and it's not like words on a page. It's a whole new language. I take a deep breath and I adjust the straps of my rucksack because all the tins are pressing into my shoulders and making them creak.

I hold the map up to the misty light and I try to imagine the lines as the paths splayed out to each side of us and I try to put myself on the paper and follow the black trails through the swirls and the swoops of ink. The hazelnut house is behind us. The seed house is in front of us. In between is the curve of a river and the scribble of a forest.

I turn slowly and I see the scrabble of the hillside beneath us where we climbed up to find the house. Not that way. Left or right or straight on. I turn again. To the left there is a forest but no river. To the right there is a river but I can't see trees. Just scrubby wild grass that hisses in the wind. Straight on. I squint through the halflight. The sky is heavier than earlier and the clouds roll like smoke. There is a dark shadow in the distance that looks like eyelashes brushing the edge of the sky. Trees circling mountains. I can't see the river but I turn again and follow its snaking shape and it curves and twists and it slips off and away and into the distance towards the branch-lined foot of the mountains. It looks to me like we need to cross over their biting teeth and emerge on the other side into a new valley.

This way I say. *Definitely this way. We'll find the seed house first, I think.*

Rey rolls her eyes and mutters something and it was the way she was pointing all along but I had to make sure. I still don't understand this place.

As we set off I feel the strange spiking pinprick of eyes on me. But all around me there is mist and nothingness and a path that winds slowly towards the dark loom of a mountain.

Chapter 42

We walk along and Rey points out more tangles of bushes and flower buds and the occasional skyshadow of a faraway bird. She sees life everywhere here and I try to find it too but it's not as easy as Rey makes it look.

She might have walked this way, you know says Rey as she trails her fingers through the tall grass either side of us. *She might have touched this grass and felt this earth. Isn't that kind of amazing?* She bends down and scoops a handful of mud, which is a bit weird but whatever makes her happy.

Yeah maybe I say and before I can stop the story I make it true in my head and I see her tall and elegant and red-haired and walking through the grass with a flower behind her ear and a trail of foxes streaming behind her like velvet. I like the way it looks. I like that I'm here now and maybe she was here once and maybe she still is and all the jigsaw pieces fit together in a way they never have before. We're all in the picture. It's starting to feel complete.

Rey checks the map again and leads us through another swirling field of grass and tight-flowered buds and up ahead is the seed house and how easy was that? We're starting to know this place, I think. We're starting to get it. We're starting to be free.

Chapter 43

The seed house is a bit bigger than the hazelnut house but it's not quite as cosy. There is no rug on the floor and the table is missing a leg so that it has to rest against a wall or it'll fall over. The fireplace looks like something might have been nesting in it and I nervously nudge the shredded straw and bed sheets with the poker but nothing scurries out and away into the shadows except clouds of dust and ash.

Rey lights a fire and I make tea and fill our water bottles and it feels like we have a routine that fits just us and it's brilliant. Rey grins at me as she looks at the tins and says *What do you want for tea? I'll cook* and we choose exactly what we want to eat and we sit together on the stone floor and eat bubbling stew right from the pan and afterwards we scoop hot yellow custard with our fingers and it streaks our faces.

Imagine she was a chef I say. *Imagine she could cook us any meal we asked for and she found all the right ingredients here in the wildlands and she could forage and find anything at all and every meal was cooked exactly right.*

Imagine she foraged Rey says.

Yes! I say and I find all the right words. *Imagine she could make fruit pies and ice cream and eclairs and those croissants with chocolate inside and milkshakes with whipped cream piled high and imagine she taught us how to make them as well.*

Imagine she was a wilder says Rey but I shake my head and I keep talking about pastries and lemonade and it's the best time we've ever played.

Chapter 44

The next morning we get ready and set off early into the foxlight. It's chilly and the light turns grey. We walk towards the mountain through valleys that are burned bronze with dead grass. Once we see the shadow of a bird skating through the mist but then it disappears again and it was so quick I think it must have been a cloud. We stop to eat fistfuls of chocolate and we share a cold tin of tomatoes that taste fresh and bright. I have to slice the tin open with Rey's little knife because we left the opener behind but it doesn't matter because I get there in the end. The wind blows but I am starting to like the chill on my cheeks and the air tastes as fresh as the tomatoes. Rey and I keep grinning at each other and we share looks that mean *We're on our way, we're going to find her, we're going to find our story*. My blood buzzes with nerves and excitement and worry.

The grass starts to fade into dark earth and the path twists upwards in a corkscrew that winds through the crags of the mountainside. It gets harder and harder to walk without the muscles in my legs screaming in protest. We are carried higher and higher out of the valley and up the side of the mountain. We rise with the wind.

I see the space spread out beneath us and I feel a bit sick. The path gets narrower. After a little while we have to go single file and one side of the track slopes away into nothing but air and wind and I feel even more sick.

Rocks and stones crumble away beneath our boots and slide down off the mountain. I don't hear them land but I can't stop imagining that it's Rey slipping and falling and whirling through the empty air to the hungry ground below. My jaw is clenched so tight that my teeth squeak together with every careful step. I watch my scuffed boots and my arms splay out so I can try to keep my balance.

The air nips and bites and the clouds growl. I can barely see the ground and my feet keep finding nooks and crannies in the earth and I stumble again and again. My ankles knock together and I can feel bruises bursting into blue on my knees. I can't even see my hand when I hold it out in front of me. I am terrified.

I stumble to the ground and I shout with fear and my hands hit something wet and smooth and soft and sticky and I scramble back without thinking how stupid that is but somehow I stay away from the edge. Spread on the ground are bones. The skeleton of something that was once heart-beating and strong and full of blood and muscle and teeth and is now being swallowed by the ground. I can see a mass of feathers made heavy by blood and I shriek and pull back and wipe my hands desperately on a bare patch of earth. The air is filled with the scent of something rotten and forgotten. Death.

In a rush of revulsion and fear and teeth-chattering cold I want to go back to the hazelnut house. Back to somewhere warm and safe. Back to stories.

The wildness in me has been rotting away. It has scattered in the dull earth, falling away from me piece by piece like shedding a skin. I've been trying and I've been pretending and I've been caught up in tiny beautiful moments that felt just right but everything else has just been wrong and now I feel raw.

Life and death are inches apart and overlapping and snapping at my heels. The bright buzz from a few hours before has faded and instead terror is lapping inside me. The wildlands change and roll and shift and I can't keep my grip on them. I can't find my stride. One moment they're brightly coloured and beautiful and the next they stink of death and fear. They're too huge and too dangerous and too unknowable and I am lost inside them.

Up ahead Rey is practically skipping. I call out to her and I try to keep my voice low because I'm worried the strength of it might topple one of us off the mountainside. But Rey doesn't hear and she carries on prancing and I swallow a lump of fear but it lodges in my throat.

I watch Rey skip with nimble feet that seem to know the ground like an old friend. Feet that understand the wild. Feet that belong here.

And then I fall.

167

Chapter 45

The air rips apart. I slip through it like water through fingers. Down. Down. Down.

My heartbeat is louder than the storm.

I squeeze my eyes tight shut and salt tears escape and burn on my wind-bitten cheeks.

I am falling with the rain.

It's taking the tiniest snatch of a second and it's taking forever.

I am not part of the world any more.

I'm falling through time and life.

And then the wind catches me.

It can feel it, lifting me, grabbing me, holding me in its spiked fingers, ripping at my skin and my hair, gobbling me up, swallowing me whole.

I open my eyes.

I am caught in a gorse bush. Its teeth snare my

168

ankles and bite into my trousers. Beads of blood flush red around my wrists. I stare upwards at empty sky and down towards a muddy path ten feet below.

I can't believe how cruel this journey is.

I can't believe any mother would want this for her children.

The thread that brought me here twists and snaps.

I want the mother I made for us, the one I spun with my words and my mind and with stories and ideas that came from nothing but me.

I don't want any of this. I don't want the furious clouds and the stumbling ground and the wide snapping mouth of the wind and the wild nights that tear at my skin, I don't want the one who left her babies in the freezing winter foxlight. I don't want the one who didn't come back for us. I don't want the one who couldn't even be bothered to leave us with our names. I want to push it all away with a roar so fierce that I split the sky.

Chapter 46

I scramble and fight with the prickly gorse until it releases me from its hundreds of tiny snapping jaws and my feet scrape the ground and I fall with a thump.

Fen? Fen! Rey's voice pipes clear through the mist and suddenly she's there with her yellow hat and her wide eyes. *Oh! You're all right! I thought for a second something terrible had happened.*

It has! I shout and I don't mean to be so loud but the words punch out of me. *Something terrible has happened! I fell off a mountain!*

But you're fine says Rey and she reaches out her hand to help me up and her face is relief and concern and happiness. *You're OK. You're not hurt.*

I am hurt! I roar and I hold out my bloody wrists and the gorse's pinprick bites that tattoo my arms and

I point at my tender ankle. *I am hurt* I say more quietly.

Poor Fen says Rey and she squats down next to me. *But it's just scratches. Just little scratches. We'll get to the next house and we'll wash them out and we'll get you warm and we'll carry on. It's all going to be OK.*

She uses some water from her bottle and sluices it on to my cuts. It stings and I close my eyes because they sting too.

It's OK says Rey again. *It's all going to be OK.* She is calm and gentle and her hands are soft and careful and all of a sudden I can't stand it and I can't stand to be touched and I can't stand her soft words and I can't stand this place and I can't stand anything at all any more and I explode.

Stop it I shout. *Stop it! Stop it! I don't need you to take care of me. I don't need anyone to take care of me. Just leave it alone, leave me alone.* I bat Rey's hand away with mine and she rocks backwards on her haunches and blinks.

I'm just trying to help says Rey and her voice is harder than I've ever heard it.

171

I don't need your help I say. I don't need anyone's help. I can't believe I started to think I did. I can't believe I started to imagine how it could be. I can't believe I let stories take shape.

OK, well get up on your own then and we'll keep going Rey says and she doesn't look at me as she speaks.

To find our mother I say sarcastically and Rey looks startled.

Yes she says and each word is short and cut with a knife. *That's why we're here. To find our mother.*

I throw my scratched arms out wide into the snapping wind of the gathering storm.

What kind of a mother would leave her babies here, Rey? What kind of a mother wouldn't fetch us herself if she wanted us back? What kind of a mother would leave us in the first place? She's not a fox whisperer or a gem collector or even just a good person. She's not going to bake us cakes or take us on adventures or teach us how to live out here. She left us. She left us in the cold and she left us with nothing at all.

My voice roars and I shout into wild wind that's

pulling and tugging at feelings that have been buried deep inside me. Feelings that are as hard and sharp as conkers and if you tear away their protective spiky skin then the truth shines out bold and bright. Because I have never thought about the truth of her before, the truth underneath all the stories and the imaginings and the questions. And now it is everywhere around me, sewn into the seams of earth beneath me and breathed into the bruised clouds above me.

Rey stares at me. She is bonewhite.

I don't know she says. *But that's why we're here. To find her. To find out. That's why we came.*

Don't be such an idiot, Rey. Have you ever even stopped to think about any of this? Why would you want to know, why would you want to find her now? When she's stayed away, stayed hidden somewhere we could die trying to find?

Maybe she's not what I thought she was says Rey and her voice rises with the wind. *We don't know what she is, we don't know if she's kind or cruel, we don't know if she's what we imagined or not or if she's somewhere in between. But I'm going to find out. I want to find out.*

173

No, Rey, we can't. I don't want to wander forever through storms to find her. I want to be free, don't you get it? That's why I came here. This isn't freedom. This is just stupid. Chasing a story, chasing someone who doesn't want us. I don't want it. I want to be free.

Rey stands up and the storm crackles behind her and she is electric in its light.

You don't know what you want she says quietly and my mouth falls open because how can she say that? She's the one who stopped me having what I wanted. And she's the one who is still stopping me being free.

Rey is still talking.

It's up to you whether you come with me. But if you want freedom, you've got it. You go and find that. But I'm going to go and find out once and for all. I came out here for a reason and I'm not afraid of finding out the truth for certain. Not like you. You're the one always hiding in wild stories and never thinking what might be real. I'm not afraid.

The storm stretches and roars and the sky cracks open and the rain is as sharp as ice. Lightning makes the mist glow blue and luminous and the thunder shakes the ground and echoes through my bones and I stay on the trembling earth and watch Rey walking away until the mist swallows her up.

Chapter 47

I stay on the ground with the storm and my thoughts
swirling around me until my bones are cracking with
fury and cold. Rey has left me. All alone on the side
of a mountain and how could she just walk away, step
into the mist and disappear without me, how could
she do that to me? My blood burns.

I struggle up and my ankle wobbles uncertainly. I
take a few strange steps with no one by my side and
I put my hand in my pocket and I pull out the map. I
realise with a little jolt that Rey doesn't have the map
but I fold that feeling away because she's made her
choice. I don't need her. How dare she tell me I don't
know what I want. I've always known what I want.

I look at the map and it's bleary with rain but I can
see that I'm not too far from the flower house. I hope
Rey doesn't decide that's where she's heading too. I

feel that little jolt again when I think about her wandering homeless through the wildlands but I squash it down again. It was her choice.

I trace my finger along the inky lines of the map. I'll go to the flower house and spend the night there. I'll have a big supper by the fireside and I'll be cosy and warm and then I'll set off back to the Light House tomorrow. Everything will be fine. Everything is fine.

I keep repeating that in my head, in time to the thumping beat of my boots on the wet and frozen earth. The words stop meaning anything at all. They stop me thinking anything at all until each thump starts to sound like her name.

Rey.

Rey.

Rey.

Stupid Rey. Stupid, stupid Rey. I've always been the brave one. I'm not afraid of the truth. As soon as I think that I remember the soft edges of the mother I was piecing together. How I made her what I wanted her to be. How I wouldn't think about her at all

177

otherwise. But that's because I was thinking about the wildlands, because I was thinking about Rey.

But I don't need Rey. I don't need anybody. I'm fine on my own. I could find the hazelnut house again. Maybe that's where I belong and that's where I can stay. Out of the cruel winds and biting lands and inside cosy by a fire. Just me. Free.

The storm slices through me. The map is curling and wet even though I've tried to keep it dry, but I think I'm getting closer. I have to be getting closer. But everything looks the same and different all at once. The mountain path slopes up and then down. It twists and turns and the rain cloaks the light and I don't know which way is before and which is after. I am turned around and I see a rotten tree stump and then I'm sure I see it again five minutes later but surely that's impossible because I've just kept walking straight on haven't I and how could I be going in circles and will I ever find where I need to be and the cold is fire on my skin. The rain has soaked every inch of me. It makes my socks squeak against my boots and my ankle pulses with each step. The pain flashes

178

hot and cold, hot and cold and I start to limp. I drag myself on and water rushes from my clothes in tiny rivers. My blood hums with pain and frost.

Dusk is blooming and I'm sure I'm going to have to sink into the damp earth and spend the night in the dark wild until I see the shape looming ahead.

A house.

Chapter 48

It's not the flower house. I don't know how I've got turned around and mixed up but I don't care one bit. It's a house. It has a roof and walls and it isn't open to the sheeting rain and even though my ankle screams I run towards the door. There's a bird carved above the door but I can't tell what kind it is because I don't really know any birds. It looks sharp and cruel and it makes me shudder. Rey would know. I throw open the door and the hinges scream into the quiet dusk.

Inside is instantly not the same as the hazelnut house. Instead of cupboards of neatly stacked tins and carefully arranged books everything is flung haphazardly on filthy open shelves. Books with their covers bent back and old socks and pencil stubs and crusted plates and an ashtray filled with grey grit and the wrinkled stubby fingers of old cigarettes. There is a small table but no chairs and only a few spindly logs scattered by the fireplace. There isn't a rug to sit on in front of the flames and the stone floor is stained and smeared like it's never once been mopped. The air is thick with the scent of something damp and rotten. No one has taken any care when they lived here. I move cautiously through the room and great clouds of dirt and dust plume around me. I look at the food supplies. The tins are dented and there are only a handful. Most of the labels have faded or peeled off. There is no tin opener anywhere and the sink is ringed with layers of grease and grime. It smells worse than the rest of the room and I run some water to try to rinse away the worst of the stink but the tap spurts something blackened and foul. I gag and step away and my ankle protests.

I limp to a wobbly chair and I take off my sodden boots and peel back my soaking sock and trouser leg and I see a galaxy of bruises swirling on my skin. I try to use a tiny bit of precious bottle water to clean a small cut but I just spill it everywhere and I swear with words Lissa hates and there's no one to hear them.

Something white and bright catches my eye by the window. A flash of bone. I limp over with my still dirty ankle dripping water into my already wet sock. All along the window sill are sharp-beaked skulls. Death and rot are everywhere here just like on the mountain and I can feel it curling and creeping in the corners. Further along the sill are whole bird skeletons picked clean of flesh. Hollow eyed and forever flightless. I shudder. The hazelnut house felt like a home. I don't know what this place feels like but I can't wait to leave.

Chapter 49

The wood here is too wet to burn. I can't start a fire. I sweat and I swear and I scream but the flames won't lick the kindling to light and life and I am so cold that my teeth chatter and I think they might break. I wrap my arms around my knees and hug myself tight but it doesn't help. I try to eat some chocolate but it crumbles in my quivering mouth and I'm not hungry anyway.

The silence around me grows and twists and the night stretches and yawns and the shadows loom.

I close my eyes tight and I imagine.

I try to imagine I'm OK on my own.

But I can't.

Chapter 50

The next morning Rey is not curled into me. There is no little oval dent where her small body has left the lightest imprint on the straw. The mattress beside me is cold. It is the strangest feeling in the whole wide world and I can't stand being inside and alone for a second longer and I leap up even though my ankle is still tender and I grab my bag and I burst out through the wooden door into the yellow morning light. The storm has blasted away the mist and picked the sky clean of clouds and for the first time I can see bright blue sky. The sunlight changes everything. Everything is cleaner and newer and fresher. I can see the shape of a bird high above and it arcs and swoops and it's so beautiful I want to reach up and touch it and I turn to tell Rey because I can't remember if we've even see a bird like this before and I want to store up every single feather so we can tell Robin, but the space next to me is empty and of course she's not here. Of course she's not.

Chapter 51

I am lonely. I try the word in my mouth and it's a hollow howl of sound. Lonely. I've never been lonely before. I've never been alone before. I have only ever had noise and chaos and music and children and Lissa and Rey.

But this is how it is now. I've chosen it. I've chosen to be lonely. And the word shakes my bones a little more every time I think it and I draw my arms around me and I try to hold myself close.

The air here is bitter and the skulls are gleaming behind the window glass. I can't stay here. If I am going to be lonely I have to do it somewhere else. I'll find my way back to the hazelnut house. That's the best plan I've got. It's the only plan I've got.

I step forward on to the stormfresh earth and there's no one by my side and it feels so strange I take a sharp breath that squeezes my lungs tight.

I look at the map again and my fingers trace the steps to the hazelnut house. The ink has bled from the rain last night but I think I can follow the lines. There are so many different paths and they all feel wrong. It's overwhelming. All this choice. All down to me.

I choose one that seems the shortest and I start to walk. Alone.

I stomp and stamp in a rhythm that tries to drown out my thoughts. But I can't push my feet hard enough into the frosted ground. I can't thump my boots with the right speed. My thoughts are twisting and growing like vines.

What if Rey has found our mother
                    What if she loves Rey
What if it's just the two of them
                 What if Rey doesn't love me
                    What if I'm lonely forever
                 What have I got left now
No wild dream
            No mother
                 No Rey

Each step is harder and harder and I want to thump down on to the ground and sink into the soft earth and let plant roots grow around me and flowers dance along my skin and never have to think or move again.

Chapter 52

I come to the river. It glitters and snakes and sparkles in the surprise sun and I am not sure it's meant to be here and I wasn't looking for it and I must be lost and of course I am because this is how things are out here. Impossible and cruel. I get out the map but the more I look at it the less sure I am. The rain has made it too hard to understand and I don't know what's river and what's path and what's been washed away forever.

I look up and down the riverbank. It cuts everything in half. I can't see a place where it ends and I can't see a place where it begins and my ankle throbs and I have to be on the other side of it because in the distance when I squint I can see the tips of the hills that shelter the hidden hazelnut valleys. Unless I want to wind back and try and find another way, I have to get across. The thought of turning round and round and stumbling down paths and through bracken and moss and mud and never finding the right way makes my heart slip and sink. I have to go forward. I have to cross.

I try to see a crossing place but there's nothing but shining water that shows me the sky. There aren't even rocks or pebbles to scramble across, sliding my feet over their slippery skin. I'll have to go through.

I can't swim.

And you're always afraid says a tiny voice in my head but I shout at it to shut up and I shout in real life and a watchful crow startles and flaps its ragged wings.

I have to get across.

I am not going to be afraid any more.

Chapter 53

The riverbanks are steep and muddy and studded with sharp stones. I pick up a stone and I throw it down into the water to try to see how deep it is. But the stone is washed away in an instant before it has a chance to sink to the murky bottom. I gulp and the air is wet. But I don't have a choice.

I think I remember Robin saying that clothes and shoes weigh you down and you should always take them off in the water but the cold air snarls and I can't imagine peeling off my layers and letting the river water bite my skin. So I roll up the legs of my trousers even though there's no point because the water will lash up to my thighs. I keep my boots on because I don't know what's on the bottom of the river but I don't want it to find my toes.

The water is so cold that I shout again and another

crow panics itself into an inky burst of feathers. It cuts through to my bones and makes them sharp and searing. I am only up to my ankles and I'm already trembling so hard that my teeth are knocking and cracking together in my jaw. All the hairs on my body stand on end and the cold shoots through me like fire.

It is impossible to take a step forward. I am frozen in a bonesharp body with a hammering heart. I can't make my limbs do anything. I'm not even sure if my feet still exist. I can't see them. I can't feel them. I can't make them do what I want them to do.

I step forward. My boot shucks and sinks in the river mud and I nearly step right out of it but I manage to keep my foot flat inside it and I throw my arms out for balance. I wobble but actually my boots being glued to the riverbed helps me and I stay upright. I have to fight to free them and that makes me weave like a ribbon in the wind.

The water is rising. First it was licking my ankles and now it is hungrily lapping at my knees with an icy needle tongue. I can feel it wrapping around me and trying to pull me into its heart. I brace my knees and

192

I keep wading through and I look straight ahead at the other bank.

Water drips off me and out of me like I am a storm cloud and my mood is the same. The air feels almost warm compared to the water but I am still soaked through and covered in slime. I feel a wave of fury roll off me like the river water.

I am only halfway across.

I take each step carefully. I wish I had something to brace myself against and stick into the water every time I moved forward. I wish I'd thought to find a big branch. I didn't plan this well at all and I'm soaked and stinking.

My foot catches on something smooth and slippery. Something sharp slices at me and I know there is pain but it is muffled and numbed by the cold and the shock. My whole body slides from beneath me before I even notice something is wrong. There is a moment where I'm suspended in mid-air and I can see the sky and the river and the bank beyond but they've all shifted and changed position and I think *That's odd* and then the water crashes up to meet me.

I am in the river and I am part of the river and I am not part of the river and it is trying to spit me out.

The water splinters me. I think I have actually shattered into a million pieces and I am just shards of Fen floating down the river towards the fast-foaming current round the bend. Then a rush of water hits me and I realise I am still in one piece but I am also knocked down on my back in the middle of a furious ribbon of river.

I try to flip over so I can scrabble to my knees and push myself up but everything is so slippery and it's like I am made of weeds and water too and I slide and splash and I can't get a grip anywhere or on anything. The river flows into my eyes and my nose and I cough and I splutter and I can't get enough air. The water is so loud and it's all I can hear and all I can see and all I can feel. I've only been down for seconds and already all the strength I ever had has fizzled out and died just like our first fires in the wild.

I imagine all the people who went to the wildlands and never came back just like Marl said and I imagine their skeletons beneath my feet and their bone-withered hands reaching up for me and tugging at my boots and pulling me towards them and pulling me to the airless riverearth that is their home now and I can feel their fingers grasping for me and I scream as my head breaks the surface and then I am pulled under again.

I try to heave myself up and my hands claw uselessly at the water and I don't have the strength and whenever I think I'm free of the current I am gripped and grabbed and tumbled again.

There's no way out.

The only way is down down down.

I close my eyes. I let the water wash over me and pull me and spin me until the world is nothing.

I'm going to sink into the riverbed and it's going to swallow me whole and no one will ever know what happened to me and my story will be nothing but questions and I'll never eat sugared porridge by the fireside or tell stories under the covers or play cards on a wintery afternoon or sing along to the piano or moonwatch from our window ever again. I'll never see Lissa or Robin or Zaki or Alex or Jasmine or Alice or Inigo ever again. I'll never see Rey ever again. I've been

195

searching for my story but they were it, they were a beautiful tangled chaotic scribble of people and love and fury and joy and stories and dreams and I never even stopped to think how much colour they gave me and I never stopped to think how your story is not the one you tell yourself but something that shifts and shapes itself around a beautiful terrifying mess of lives and people and how I should never have been searching for just one arrow-straight path because that's not what a story is and stories loop and turn and curve and twist but there is always something that stays the same. Something that guides you through the chaos.

Rey.

And then I see Rey. Rey's face, so careful and brilliant and bright and brave and full of my whole world. The chaos and the mess and the love and the warmth and the freedom and she is my fixed star and my true story and I love her and I have to do this for her.

I am not going to give her up.

And my desperate hands find a knotty root of something twining its way through the riverbed and it's enough to keep me steady enough to let me roll myself over and then my desperate foot finds the grip of gravel on the riverbed and it's enough for me to push myself to my knees and that's enough for me to lever myself up and with a surge of water and swearing and mud I am upright and standing in the flow of the river.

And I turn around in the very middle of the river and I don't take my eyes off the bank because I know exactly where I need to go.

The fox house.

Chapter 54

When I scramble out of the water my clothes are wetter than they've ever been and I am heavy with the guts of the river. Every single fibre and sinew and nerve and atom in my broken body wants to stop but I don't care. I could be on fire or covered in biting ants and stinging bees and I wouldn't stop.

I have to find Rey.

I wheeze on the riverbank and I cough up lungfuls of water and it splatters my boots. My stomach churns and cramps and I heave and heave and heave. Each spasm is like electricity and my face is raw and wet with river and tears. I let the river roll out of me and when it's all gone I still heave but now the tears are winning.

But I have to find Rey.

She's right. I've been hiding in stories. I've been telling them because they're easier than what might be true. And when I thought about what might be true I let her go into the mouth of the wildlands alone. Protecting myself from what comes next was more important than protecting Rey.

I'm a terrible sister.

She is so brave.

I'm a coward.

I have to find her.

I have to make this right.

But I don't know which way to go and I pull out the map but it's nothing but a wash of blue now and the river and the trees are swirled together and right and left don't matter on there any more. I squeeze my eyes tight closed and try to remember the shapes on the map and water trickles from between my eyelids and I don't know if it's from the river or from me.

I have to find Rey.

I try to see the map in my mind but every time I try to hold the image still it swoops away. I screw up my face and I close my eyes and I conjure it again and again but every single time it drifts out of focus just when I think I can hold it steady. I think I had to go straight on from the river and keep the trees on my right. But what if it was my left?

A sound pierces the sky.

It's terrible and beautiful all at once. A strange screeching that comes from deep inside.

My first thought is it must be Rey and there must be something very wrong because that's not a noise I've ever heard her make and it sounds like she's dying. I whirl around and try to see her in the clumps of dull wildflowers or the dark prints of trees but she isn't anywhere.

I call her name and the sound comes again and then I see it.

Silk and sinew and fire and earth.

The fox.

She opens her mouth and she makes her wonderful brutal sound again and then she turns and slips away and over the hill with the trees on her right.

She came.

She came back.

Chapter 55

I have a surge of energy sparking inside me because the fox came back.

I clamber over the brow of the hill and the land rolls out in front of me. It's different this side of the river. The sky seems lower but maybe that's because the sun has disappeared and the clouds are billowing again. The land is darker and there aren't so many bursts of flowers or twists of green grasses dancing together. It looks wilder and more abandoned than what was before. The soil is wetter and it sucks at my boots and I sink into its springiness and pull my feet out before I'm eaten by the earth.

Every so often I see the spring of the fox's tail bristling among slender stalks of straw grass. Her coat is bright against the dull colours of this new wildland. I remember Marl telling us the land was dead and how it hadn't seemed real when we'd first arrived. But every word is right and true now.

The fox is appearing less frequently now. The dirt-rich musk that rolls off her fur is fading. I want to stamp with frustration. I peer towards the angry jagged teeth of the mountains and over to the skeletons of trees in the distance, but she's nowhere to be seen.

I shudder but my teeth are already chattering and my body is shivering in my soaked clothes and the wool of my jumper is weighing me down so it doesn't make much of a difference. I just feel it zip up my spine like a spider. My fingers are dusky and purplish and they remind me of Rey when she gardens and I feel a lurch of loss because she's out here and blue and alone and I wish wish wish we were back in the Light House and back by the fire and back listening to Robin tell us pigeons mate for life and Alice trying to braid our hair and back somewhere warm and safe.

But Rey doesn't feel the cold like I do, I think. She doesn't mind the cold. I say the words out loud and I march along to their beat.

Rey doesn't feel the cold.

Rey doesn't mind the cold.

Rey knew what to do out here.

Rey understands this place.

Rey is brave.

I have to be brave too.

If I keep saying the words and I keep their steady rhythm then I don't have to think about Rey being alone and I don't have to think about not knowing where she's gone and I don't have to think about how I made all of this happen.

Rey knew what to do out here.

Rey understands this place.

And maybe now I do too.

Chapter 56

My legs are aching and my blisters feel round and raw. I sit down with a thump even though stopping feels wrong but I haven't seen the fox in forever. I feel almost hurt and confusion fizzes.

Why would she come back and then disappear again?

You know the answer, I think to myself. You know why. Because she's just a wild animal doing what wild animals do. Nothing more. I spun a story from her but she is wild and strange and I can't know her or understand her outside of those words. She doesn't make sense. She's not meant to because this isn't as simple as a story. This is real and I can't imagine and make her fit.

There's just one thing that I know and it's Rey.

My clothes are still damp and stiff with cold but

for a moment I forget. I forget everything and I just sink into the wild space. But the moment doesn't last long enough and Rey pops bright into my mind and the elbows of my jumper drip.

I'll light a fire. I'll keep myself warm for a little while.

So I gather sticks and leaves and I take the skinny logs from my backpack but they're soaked through and they won't work at all. They splinter my finger and I hurl them into the grass in fury and I take a deep cold breath and instead I find some fat twigs and they'll have to do. I find some green sponges of moss and add that too because I remember what Rey said back when we built the first fire. It feels forever ago and she feels so very far away. But she feels a tiny bit closer when I think about the fact we're both out here in the very same space and I imagine her building a fire and cooking something tinned and horrible and warm over its flames.

I poke the firelighters into little gaps in the pile. I strike a hissing match and the flame jumps and multiplies and creeps and grows and I am so happy Rey told me to take the firelighters and so guilty when I think of how I rolled my eyes because they weren't how I thought this should be. Soon the warmth is growing in me too, a little seed that burns and blooms. I eat some dusty chocolate. I make porridge and eat it hot and creamy with my fingers right from the little pan.

Chapter 57

I feel so small and alone. There is no second heartbeat, no quiet wild sister. We have never been apart for more than minutes. I keep opening my mouth to talk to empty air. It feels like I have been ripped in two and my edges are jagged. I remember Rey's paperback book flapping in the breeze, story torn in two. I wonder if Rey is feeling the same, or whether she's bouncing through the wildlands and alive with the wonder of it all. She was so happy here even when I thought it was terrifying and terrible. Maybe she prefers it like this. Alone. Without me complaining and telling her things aren't true and pulling apart her hopes.

Acid splashes inside me. I caused this and I have to find her and try to fix it, even if she never wants to speak to me again.

I try to remember how I used to see the wildlands when I gazed out of my window at the home. How they shifted and changed as the sun and moon crossed over the sky and how their wildness was like a secret I was desperate to be told. I remember the stories I created. The worlds I built out here and how I imagined it would be. Freedom.

I close my eyes.

I imagine. I shape the story of the wildlands in my mind. If I'm going to find her, I have to find a way to survive out here. I have to find a way to make it mine too. Trying to follow Rey's exact steps will never work. I need to trust myself and find a way to trust the wildlands. I can't tame them. I can't make them safe and easy. But I can try to understand them. I can accept the truth of them. I can try to find how I fit into them and their story. Not the other way around.

Just like I have to do with Rey. Just like I have to do with our mother.

I open my eyes and I look again.

The light is fading slowly, dissolving into the sky. Saltbright stars are beginning to scatter. I look up and see the whole night stretching above me. The stars I gazed up at that first night with Rey when the fire burned bright just like this one. And then I see it. I see it without any help, without having to struggle and squint and stare at a diamond-studded sky. It is standing proud among the swirling ice and fire of the night. Always there, fixed and blinking in a chaotic cosmos. The North Star.

The starlight makes the brown earth shimmer and shine. It stops being dark and cold and cruel and it becomes something soft to hold me while I rest. Tree branches that twist like bones instead sweep gently against the clouds. The jagged teeth of mountains soften into something dusky and blurred melting into the sky. There is still danger there but it's far away and I'm right here.

I watch the world around change from day to night. The colours shift before my eyes and I start to see new shapes and shadows fall. I hear a single bird call softly from far away, and then another answers with its song. I touch the dry tendrils of grass and I see moonlight bathing tiny flowers in its milky spell.

Their petals glow like velvet. There are wild secrets hidden everywhere. There is beauty and danger and wildness and home. And there is always the North Star.

And in the morning I choose my own path towards the fox house and I don't know if it will work but I have to try.

Chapter 58

I walk for most of the morning and the day is bright and cold. I choose paths that feel right and that slope towards the edges of the map in my memory. I see things that Rey would see for me, like jewelled berry spheres and dark holes dug by frantic paws. My ankles twist and stumble sometimes but I dust my knees and I keep going. I keep my eyes on the land and it keeps its eyes on me.

I am walking towards her. I will walk for as long as it takes and I won't stop. I find my way and I don't trust the lands but I trust myself. I am in control and not in control and I am afraid and I am brave and that's what being wild and free is.

By the afternoon the earth beneath my feet is getting wetter and wetter. The marsh is beginning. The sky hasn't cracked open yet but the mists are starting to gather and cloak the light. But I can see the shape of a house in the distance. I remember the map. River then valley then marsh then fox house. I'm nearly there.

The house rises from the marshland like a looming beast. Its angles are sharp against the sky and it is real and it is there and I stop because walking towards it is walking towards something that I can't ever unknow and there is fear wriggling up my spine and through my blood and it turns me into a statue and I can't take another step.

Then there is a snap of leaves and a crunch of ground and I whirl round and I look for the rush of red fur and the endless dark eyes and the salted tang of earth and wild but it's not our fox.

A cool hand slips into mine and Rey is there. My brilliant, brave, wild, North Star sister. She's covered in mud and her edges are sharp and the sun is bright behind her and she has leaves in her hair and mud everywhere and her cheeks have been brushed pink by the wind and I can see every detail of her face and I can smell her flowersoil scent and it's perfect and my sister is here and the world is piecing itself back together again and I have so many questions but that's not for right now so instead I squeeze her hand in mine so tight that I worry my bones will crack but Rey just squeezes back and says *Shall we go in then?*

We'll find the truth together.

Chapter 59

The house is the same as the others except for the fox carved above the door. Its lines are so familiar to me now and yet there's something I don't like about seeing our fox trapped in stone like this, frozen forever.

I take a deep breath and I pull the door in a creak of ancient hinges.

Rey's fingers tremble in mine.

We step forward and we go through the gaping mouth of the door and we walk inside the fox house.

It's empty.

Just like all the others.

It is grimy and dark and there is dust dancing in the air. There are the same pots and pans and firewood and tins and books and emptiness. There are framed drawings hung on nails on the walls and there is a

214

vase on the table stuffed with dried flowers that have faded pale in the low light.

There is no one here.

There is nothing here.

No one who will bake for us or hold us close or take us on adventures or who will gather us up in their arms and say my babies my babies you came back to me. No one who will even tell us who we are.

She left us in the frozen wildlands and she left us with nothing and she didn't wait for us and she didn't send for us and she didn't want us.

And that's the truth of it.

And it's so whole and huge and new and familiar and terrible and it hits me like lightning and I howl into the dust-speckled air and Rey holds me tight.

Chapter 60

She didn't love us at all I hiccup and my feelings fill the whole house. This is why I didn't want the truth. This is why I wanted stories and for us to tell our own instead of trying to find hers. It's better not to know. I wipe my sleeve roughly over my eyes. *What kind of a mother does that?*

Rey is picking through the sparse shelves and not saying very much at all and I think she's in shock or maybe she hasn't forgiven me for our fight and the thought of that makes me cry again and I push my head between my knees and close my eyes and try to push away the world and everything is black.

Rey shakes my shoulder.

I open my eyes and see her blurry shape and she's trying to show me something but my eyes won't focus.

Look breathes Rey and I blink away a wash of tears
and she's holding out a notebook.

Chapter 61

The notebook is yellowed and curled with age and dust and sunlight. The cover might once have been red but it's washed pink by time and it's stained with marks that I hope are tea and coffee. The spine is cracked like someone opened it and closed it like a chest.

And inside is treasure.

Each page is beautiful. There are so many of them. It's a proper book but it's been made by one person and a handful of pens and soft colours. There are careful drawings of plants and flowers, each stem and petal gently shaded and shaped. Notes about how they grow best and where they grow best. The lines and bones of foxes and birds spread on to paper. A weather chart and the moon cycle and the times of sunrises across the year.

There is a more detailed map of the wildlands with little notes about how to get to each house and what the person living there was doing. Someone to help the fish live in the river water and someone to help the birds reach the skies and someone to make the plants burst into fruit and flowers. Someone to wild the foxes.

There are pages and pages on foxes. How to encourage them to breed. How to make the land theirs. How to coax them into living a life in the wildlands. How to keep them fat and fed when there is no prey for them, but how to keep them wild and free at the same time.

Hide scraps for them reads Rey and we think of Marl a million years ago back at the house.

This is a whole book of the wildlands.

This is hers says Rey. *This is her book*. And she pulls out her own notebook and she opens the pages and I see the gentle twists of plants I drew for her rising from the pages and the loops of Rey's words describing how they grow here and what they smell like. Page after page of the wildlands.

I want to say no. I want to tell Rey to stop living in stories and to stop looking for pieces that fit together and make sense and that we're never going to know more than we know now and what we know now is that she didn't care.

And then Rey turns the page of our mother's notebook.

And there we are.

Chapter 62

Two small babies. Pencil-shaded and ink-lined.

Rey's tiny face has the same dreamy moonglow and mine is dark and serious and those babies are us and I know it and so does Rey. It's a telescope looking back in time and we see ourselves.

Me and Rey.

There is nothing else on the page.

No note. No date. No little scribbled message that says who we are or what we meant. Just our faces pressed into paper and left behind in this quiet house where nobody ever goes.

Rey strokes the lines of our cheeks and she turns the page and then the next and then the next and she's searching for more of us. She's desperate and hungry for our stories and something that will tell us more, but after a few wildflowers and the time of a moonrise in July, the pages fade to blank and there is no more.

We are one page in her story.

But she kept us. She wrote us down. She drew us and she knew every line of our faces and no matter what, that means something. It might not be the perfect puzzle piece and it might not give us a perfect answer but it gives us something.

We mattered.

Is she coming back? asks Rey and the question shatters my heart because I have to tell Rey the truth and I have to say it gently and not like before, because what if Rey is like glass again and I break her into a thousand pieces?

I don't think so I say to Rey. *I don't think anyone has been here in a very long time.*

And Rey looks at the dust and the still air and she nods.

No she says. *I don't think anyone has. I think she's gone.*

And every word is as heavy as a stone, but Rey is tough and she doesn't crack.

Chapter 63

We curl together and we look at the notebook and there is a ragged edge where a page has been torn out and I think of the charcoal fox that fell from our grey blankets when Lissa found us. Rey pulls it from the inside of her notebook and even though it's creased and faded thin with age it fits right into place. I stroke the lines of our faces that were drawn with perfect care and I imagine the hand that made them and how my hand can sweep pencil into shapes just like this. Rey rubs her fingers gently along the edges of the paper like she's pulling the very fibres of it into herself. We look at the drawing that was us for a long time. Sometimes we cry and sometimes we stay silent and sometimes we start a sentence but neither of us knows how to end one. But I start to spin a new story and it feels just right.

Imagine I say to Rey. *Imagine there were two sisters who didn't have a mother. They went searching and travelled through wildlands that were full of life and death and they found strange creatures and fell from mountains and saw lightning fill the whole sky. Imagine they had a fight and they lost each other at the very edge of the world. Imagine one sister was afraid and she didn't want to find out the truth because it might hurt too much. Imagine the other sister was the bravest and boldest person that had ever existed and she wasn't afraid and she showed her sister how to be brave too. Imagine one was nearly swallowed whole but it didn't matter because they found each other again and they found truth and stories along the way. Imagine that their story didn't have a beginning or an end or even a middle. Imagine it was all just chaos and beauty and mess and wonder and wildness. But they had each other and once they had a mother who drew things like one sister and grew things like the other sister and she drew their faces and she wilded a whole land.*

Rey curls closer to me and I keep telling her the story and it's new and it's true and it's ours.

Chapter 64

We are famished and I heave pots and light fires and every single sinew and muscle and hair and fibre of me is tired. I stir the mush in a pan and I slop it into bowls and we sit together with our knees bumping and I look at the washing-up and the dying fire and the lumpy mattress and I just want to be somewhere where there is care. Rey is enough but the wildlands aren't. Not right now. Not yet. I want to be held and I want to be told when to go to bed and I want to be kept safe and warm.

I tell Rey and I wonder if the wild Rey who understands the ways of the wild will want to stay here but she just nods and says that it's time.

We'll come back, won't we? she says. *We'll come back here and we'll help make it wilder and bring it to life?*

And I say yes because I mean it and that sounds perfect.

We sleep on the lumpy mattress where our mother once spent her moonlit nights and I can't catch her scent or see the shifting outline of where her body pressed into the straw but I have Rey tangled around me and I have her smell and her weight and her tickling breath and I hold her close because she's my story.

The next morning we quietly pack what we need. We know where we're going. Rey picks up the yellowed notebook and wraps it in a tea towel and puts it in her backpack. Then she takes a sheet of paper from her blue pad and she looks into the dim sky outside and she looks down and she builds some words on the page.

We are called Fen and Rey. We live in The Light House. We are happy.

I sign my name **FEN** even though I don't think she'll ever see it but I care about Rey being happy more than anything and pressing my name into the paper makes her smile.

Then we wash up the pots and pans and we make the bed so that everything is nice for the next person and we leave the note in the middle of the table and we close the door on the fox house and we walk away from this chapter of our lives.

Chapter 65

I am worried about how we will find our way home without the map but when I say that to Rey she looks confused and says *How do you think I found the fox house? I copied the map when we found it. It would have been stupid to only have one copy of something that important. I've got loads, look.*

And she opens her backpack and shows me a folded piece of blue paper and then she opens her coat pocket and shows me another flash of blue and then another in her trouser pocket and one last slightly damp one in her sock.

Rey is a quiet kind of genius.

The journey home is simpler. It's quicker. It's calmer. We have the new map and we follow the North Star and we have each other and we have something new. We are different, together and apart.

228

We know the lands better now and we know their trickery and their cruelty and their beauty. I don't expect them to be kind and I don't expect them to look after me. We can look after each other. Rey reads our mother's notebook out loud like a story and we hear about the veins of the wildlands and how they pulse with life.

And so we see more. We notice more. We see the liquid flash of fish darting like quicksilver underneath the surface of the river. We see birds with wings that scrape against the sun. We see shining globes of berries hidden in the emerald shadows of bushes. We see the tiny tracks of rabbits' feet disappearing into tunnels that crisscross beneath our feet. There is life everywhere when you know how to look. I draw in Rey's notebook and I learn more and more.

The wildlands aren't everything I always wanted them to be when I looked out of my bedroom window and they called to me. They're so much more. They're dangerous and scary and beautiful and complicated and I will never understand them but I want to try.

There are still great patches of deadlands, but the

wilders didn't fail. Whatever they started here has grown and bloomed and turned into life. There are seeds of it in both of us and they are growing.

We play Imagine on the way home but we don't mention her. I don't think we need to do that any more. We don't need to keep her safe inside a story. We need to tell our own. We need to let it be messy and strange and wild.

Imagine we lived here when we're bigger. Imagine we made the land come alive even more. Imagine we grew vegetables and there were carrots and potatoes nestled in the soil. Imagine a flock of birds made the sky move every morning. Imagine foxes burning like fire in the dark. Imagine the air full of sound.

Rey holds the notebook like it's her heart.

We spend one night in the flower house and it's full of fat cushions patterned with petals and a big armchair with the stuffing falling out. There's a china tea set decorated with posies and we drink tea from its delicate cups and pretend to be queens. Rey reads about foxgloves and poppies and snowdrops and she finds a pack of seeds in a drawer and she says she's

230

going to take a few to plant at home and she stores them safely in her pocket.

The next night we find the fish house and it's dark and a bit smelly but very clean and there are fishing rods stacked neatly along the walls. It's right by a bend of the river and we try to fish using scraps from our tinned supper and nothing happens, but it's fun anyway and I try to forget falling in and gulping lungfuls of its freezing water. Rey reads about the right water temperature for salmon and how to make trout happy. She makes notes and I make a fire and I read a bit about mackerel so I can talk to Rey about them and I draw one for her too and I try to make its scales shine.

The sun is setting low and golden when we find the beginning and end of our journey.

A warm glow blooms over the dusking wildlands. It sweeps through the fading air and pushes shadows aside and it makes dark places bright.

We weren't brought here.

But we brought ourselves back.

We follow the path of light.

The Light House is guiding us home.

231

Chapter 66

The door flies open before we can even turn the handle and Lissa is standing there in a flood of light and tears and she pulls us to her before we can even speak or breathe and she holds us in her tight arms and we are a circle and no one wants to break the line that connects us all.

You're back you're alive oh girls my darling girls where have you been I've been so worried and Marl said you'd go to the wildlands and I thought you'd have gone forever and he's been out looking and I have been out searching and I stayed up every night in the tower looking and there wasn't a single sign and I thought well I thought ... it doesn't matter does it because you're home you're home you're home.

Her words rush out in a tumble and she sobs through them and she holds us even closer and I feel a flip of guilt because I didn't even think about Lissa being worried and I lean into her bones and I whisper that I'm sorry and Rey says it too.

Then the hall is flooded with noise and footsteps and the smell of sock soup and it must be a Sunday. Alice throws her arms around our circle and she says *You came back you came back* and Robin wriggles into Lissa's side and then Jasmine and Alex and Zaki and Alice are nestled against us all and then there is a tiny hand on my leg and I look down and there is baby Inigo and he's standing up all on his own and he's gazing up at me and his face cracks into a gummy grin and I am so lucky to be here and to have them all.

Chapter 67

Lissa makes us have hot steaming baths filled with things that smell like the ghosts of flowers. We scrub until we're pink and gleaming and we put on clean soft pyjamas and we go downstairs in our slippers and eat buttered toast by the fire and it's more delicious than I could ever have imagined. Inigo sits in my lap and I feed him fingers of toast and he gnaws on them and laughs in delight and I breathe in his babysoft smell and whisper stories into his tiny ears.

Robin wants to know every animal that we saw and Rey shows him drawings and sketches and he traces their lines with his finger and he mouths their names and he is filled with the wildland wonder too. Alice pretends she doesn't care about what we did and where we've been but she keeps asking little questions. Zaki shows me his new shiny red toy car and it feels like we've missed so much and been away forever and also not long at all because everything was the same and waiting for us.

We tell them about the wildlands. We tell them about the life out there and the death too. We tell them about the wide sky and the rolling hills and the dark mountains and the river and the fires and the mud and the thunder that rattled through our bones.

Rey and I don't tell them about our mother. We don't tell them about the fox and how we followed it into the wildlands. There are some stories that don't need to be shared. There are some stories that can stay between us like an invisible thread. Something that belongs only to us. Something we maybe don't understand right now but something that's ours. We put her notebook under our mattress and we'll maybe look at it together and we'll maybe look at it alone and we'll maybe leave it there like a quiet secret.

So people wilded the land? asks Robin and his voice

is full of wonder and I know he's thinking about all the birds and beauty that he's never seen before.

They tried I say. *It's getting there. It's growing. It's coming back to life. It's beginning again.*

Chapter 68

The others are sent to bed and Lissa sits us at the kitchen table. It is scrubbed clean and so familiar my heart aches. Rey traces the whorls and knots of the wood with her fingertip and it's like she's drawing herself back into a picture.

Lissa puts a pan of milk on the hob and lights the blue flames beneath. She pours fresh milk from a glass bottle into the pan and stirs in cocoa powder and brown sugar and the smell simmers in the air. She stands with her back to us and she mixes the hot chocolate slowly and carefully and she doesn't say a word. When she's poured the drink into three mugs she finally turns round and she comes and sits with us at the table.

Did you find what you wanted? she asks and she takes a sip and it's too hot and she pulls a face and puts the cup down.

Rey and I look at each other and I don't know what to say and neither does she because we did and we didn't and everything is tangled and complicated and clear and bright.

Fen, Rey, my loves? she asks again and our names feel so safe in her mouth because she gave them to us and they're who we always were and they're ours and hers.

We followed the fox I say. *We thought she'd lead us to our mother. Because of our beginning. Found with the foxes.* As I say it I flush red.

The foxes? She looks right at us and there's something like horror and sadness etched into the gentle lines of her face. *Oh, girls. Found with the foxes. That's a story. A story you asked for. I found you at the edge of the wildlands but there were no foxes there. Just that lovely drawing.*

We stare at her and the whole world spins. Lissa's hands wrap around the mug and as her fingers lace tightly together I see the moonflash of the scar on her wrist. I try to remember her telling us about the snap of fox teeth on her flesh. But I can't find the memory.

It's just part of the story, a path I've walked down a thousand times.

Oh, my lambs and her hands go to her mouth. *You asked, when you were tiny. You didn't have a letter and you told me to tell you a story instead and we looked at that beautiful little charcoal drawing your mother left with you and we imagined and we spun some words together and you asked for it every day and then you started to tell your own stories and it was like you gathered your own beginning. It was a story. I thought you ... I thought you knew.*

Rey and I are frozen. But somehow Lissa's words don't explode within me. They fit. They're a puzzle piece that slots right into place. They feel like I might have always known. Imagination and truth and longing and belonging, all churned up inside us both. Stories and life, their edges blurring and changing all the time.

Lissa's eyes are shining. She stands up and she pulls us into a hug that is dusted with chocolate and sugar and lemon soap and she kisses our hair and she calls us wild girls and she says she's so lucky we came back.

I always wanted to tell stories because I thought they were safer than the truth. But stories pull together truth and imagination and sometimes they help you find what you were really looking for. Our mother didn't leave us a letter or make a call to the house for someone to collect us and maybe she didn't care and maybe she did, but she did give us something. She gave us each other and she gave us the wildlands and we're part of each other and we're part of them too.

We are each other's beginnings and each other's stories and we're part of the stories of all the others here and they're part of ours. The wildlands didn't tell me the story I imagined. It was better and worse and more brilliant and more terrible. We found our own story, with all its truth and its hurt and its beauty and its wildness.

When we curl up in bed that night I pull Rey close to me and we whisper about the things we saw and we tell the stories and feel the cut of the wind and the damp of the mist and the glasscrunch of frozen grass beneath our feet and the wildness has wound its way into us and it will never leave.

Chapter 69

The season turns.

The fox fence has been taken down. Sometimes we all wander to the edge of the wildlands and sometimes we go a little further if Lissa lets us and sometimes Marl walks with us and tells us stories. Robin always comes. He sees the shadows of birds through the clouds and he tells us what they are and he tells us how they like to live. And Rey tells him the things she knows and when she talks about the wild her words fall like raindrops and she is aglow.

We have wildness in us. It runs through our blood and our bones. The wildlands are a part of us and we're a part of them and maybe one day soon we'll go back. And maybe our story will twist and turn and loop away again and we'll be thrown on to a new path.

And that's OK too. We have each other. And that's all I need to know right now.

Today, in the wild foxlight of morning Rey is in her garden and I am watching her and she is humming and happy. She is wearing the glittering cobweb scarf from the hazelnut house and it was mudsoaked and stinking but Lissa has washed it so gently and carefully that it shines in the yawning pink sun.

Rey has planted seeds from the wildlands and she's read all the books about the soil here and how to help things grow. She's taken our mother's words and planted them in the ground. Green shoots are poking their heads through the dark earth and there are buds shivering in the breeze and there are carrots spiking orange in the soil.

I sense her before I see her. A shifting of the air. A tingle on the back of my neck. Then a scent full of dark earth and bitter musk.

In the corner of my eye I see the movement. Fluid and flame.

Our fox.

She dips her head and laps from the glowing silver

242

of a puddle. Then she looks up and she sees me. Our eyes meet. She stares with unblinking amber eyes and for a moment it is just the two of us and nothing and no one else in this whole wide world and I feel that tug and that connection that makes no sense and doesn't fit with any fact I know.

Then in a movement that's swift and sure, she turns and she disappears into the fading foxlight.

Acknowledgements

A book is never just the work of one person, and this one is no different. So many people have been so kind and generous with their time and expertise. My agent, Catherine Clarke, and Michele Topham at FBA, everyone at Bloomsbury Children's, but especially Bea, Jade, Carla, Lucy, Ellen, Fliss, Isi, Stephanie, Mike, Anna and Sarah, for all their hard work and dedication. Bea, you still owe me an otter. And possibly now a fox.

I am so lucky to have such wonderful writer friends, and also to nurture such a fierce rivalry with Phil Earle. Special thanks to Ross Montgomery for always having the answer, and to Struan Murray for always having the drinks. Thanks to my parents, of course, and to my non-writer friends too.

Thanks to everyone who has been so supportive over the past few years. I am truly grateful for all the readers, teachers, librarians, parents and children who have championed my work. There have been many discussions lately about the lack of national review space, attention and recognition for children's books, but the fact that there are so many people out there dedicated to the cause gives me so much hope for the future. Let's keep shouting as loudly as we can.

I'd also like to thank Buddy Loves for Pets for removing a small goblin/whippet from my house on a weekly basis so I could actually write.

But the most thanks, as always, must go to Patrick. Thank you for everything. You are my home.

Another heartwarming and
life-affirming story awaits

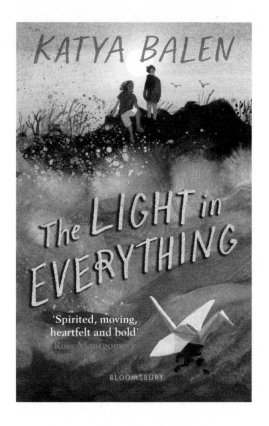

'Original, compulsive, uplifting' – *The
Times* Children's Book of the Week

'Ambitious, funny, spirited, moving, heartfelt
and bold all at once ... a force to be
reckoned with' – Ross Montgomery

AVAILABLE NOW

Turn the page for a sneak peek ...

ZOFIA

I walk Pablo along the curve of the beach. The wind is howling and it spits the sea and tangles my hair. Pablo is delighted. He is trying to stuff as much seaweed as possible into his mouth and it trails behind him as he runs, like some sort of gymnastic ribbon. Occasionally it trips him up and he rolls in a ball of weeds and paws and tail. He's going to be filthy by the time we get home. I'll let him into Dad's bedroom.

I leave Pablo to it and sit on the damp sand and watch the waves curling towards the shore. It's like the sea is breathing. I lean back so that my head crunches against the gritty ground and watch the feeble grey sky being swirled by the wind. That new strange feeling is growing shoots and leaves and I try to scream it away. I shout at the clouds and the noise bounces off the cliff and is whisked away by the wind and it's like I never made a single sound.

I don't want things to change.

TOM

We drive to a cafe. It takes quite a long time and I feel a bit green. When I get out of the car and drink great gulps of air it tastes like salt on my tongue. There are screeching cries circling above me and in the sky are a thousand gulls hunting for fish and chips. Their wings beat and graze the clouds and they bomb towards the waves chopping on the horizon. The sea makes me feel even greener. Mum gives me a smile and I swallow down the sick feeling but it's growing inside me and it's not because of the car journey.

I can see the girl and her dad sitting in the cafe and they look just like the photo Mum showed me when she told me that there were some people she'd like me to meet. Except in the photo the girl was smiling and stretched out in a star shape. Here she's curled up in a chair and furious.

Marek gets up straightaway as soon as we walk in and he leans forward like he's going to hug Mum but he stops and says *hello, Tom, I've heard so much about you, come and meet Zofia.* His voice has a lilt that sounds like the rise and fall of the waves outside. He is tall. Taller than Dad. I shrink back behind Mum and I go with her to get drinks instead of sitting down at the table with Marek and the glaring girl.

ZOFIA

When they arrive at the cafe and I meet that boy
I thought Dad had made some sort of mistake when
he told me how old he was. Eleven. Same as me
except technically I'm a month older and I have a
September birthday which means I'm nearly always
the oldest in the class and now I'm nearly the oldest
in the whole school. Anyway this boy looks like a Year
1. He is tiny and all stick arms and legs and huge eyes
and dark hair that is way too long and nibbled-down
nails. He is so pale he glows. His veins are bright blue
rivers traced on skin and his bones jut so close to the
surface that I wonder if they might break through and
if they'd even stand out against the white of his arms.
He looks like he is five or maybe six absolute
maximum. Not even nine or ten and definitely not
eleven. I can't tell if he is trembling or the slight

breeze from the door is shaking his skeleton but I roll my eyes and I practise my best glare and my best snarl and I would give anything not to be right here.

I drink my hot chocolate and Tom sits in this terrified little meek silence and for every second he stays quiet I get louder and louder just to fill the space between us with something, with some noise and chatter and words so the weight of what is happening doesn't have a chance to settle around us. The louder I am the smaller he gets. He shrinks back into his chair until it's like he is made of liquid and will soon be smoke.

Fiona tries to talk to me about school and Pablo and swimming and she even mentions Ghibli films, which makes me realise Dad must have given her some sort of Official Zofia File. I growl and glower and turn myself into a storm. No one wants to talk to me when I'm a storm. I can be a quiet furious black cloud or I can be a raging tornado but the result is the same. But Fiona keeps trying and I am also trying very hard not to let the storm take over.

I cross my fingers tight and hope very hard that we never ever have to see them again. I don't often meet

Dad's girlfriends and never their children. This must be more serious than usual but that doesn't have to mean anything. I think and hope that after seeing the Incredible Shrinking Boy that Dad will realise it was all a completely mad idea and rethink things and we can go back to the cottage and it will be me and Dad and Pablo and Frida the cat and things will stay just the same as they were before.

But when we get home Dad has a massive go at me for being *rude* and *loud* and as soon as I hear those two words I drift away and grind them up to dust and spin myself into a space far away from shouting. I can't spin myself far away enough though and I can hear some words fizzing between us.

Important

special in our lives

this is serious, I want this to work out

please, Zofia.

But I whirl away and out of the door and I sit on the sand and I let the sound of the wind and the waves curl around me until I'm calm and I watch the flags in the distance dance for me.

TOM

The night after we meet Zofia and Marek for the first time I manage twenty-two seconds. I am trying so hard but the pictures I can see in the dark won't go away. My breaths are ragged. My fingers start trembling again. My muscles shiver. I am pathetic, just like he said I was. I start folding birds. Five. Ten. Fifteen. Twenty.

Mum said Marek isn't like Dad. She promised. But how can she know? Dad could be as normal as anyone. He'd turn up to parents' evening and he'd say loudly how brilliant my work was and all the teachers would smile. He'd take me and Mum out for pizza and tell the waiter *just treating my two best people in all the world, order what you like, guys, you're worth it.* He'd buy me expensive trainers that rubbed my feet raw even though I wore them every day.

I want it to just be us. The two of us. I don't want to worry about anyone else or have to flinch and shrink at every movement. I don't want to share our space. Our lives fit us perfectly now. I don't want to go back to feeling like everything is wobbly and unsafe. And that's exactly the feeling that's creeping back into my brain and shooting through my bones.

Have you read

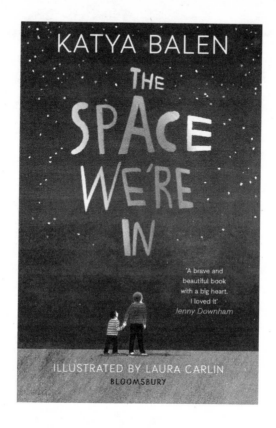

'Sensitive, heartbreaking ... a wonderful narrative voice' – *Guardian*

'It's ferocious and it's visionary' – Kevin Crossley-Holland

AVAILABLE NOW

And also by Katya Balen

Winner of the Yoto Carnegie Medal 2022

'A very special new addition
to the shelf ... deserves classic status' –
The Times Children's Book of the Week

AVAILABLE NOW